Slut?

Slut?

KERRY COHEN HOFFMANN

SIMON AND SCHUSTER

SIMON AND SCHUSTER

First published in Great Britain in 2006 by Simon & Schuster UK Ltd
Africa House, 64-78 Kingsway, London WC2B 6AH
A CBS Company

Originally published as *Easy* in 2006 by Simon & Schuster Books for Young Readers
an imprint of Simon & Schuster Children's Division, New York

A CIP catalogue record for this book is available from the British Library.

This book is a work of fiction. Names, characters, places and incidents are either
products of the author's imagination or are used fictitiously. Any resemblance to
actual events or locales or persons, living or dead, is entirely coincidental.

ISBN: 1-416-92629-1
EAN: 9781416-926290

1 3 5 7 9 10 8 6 4 2

Printed and bound in Great Britain by Cox & Wyman, Reading, Berkshire

For girls everywhere

ACKNOWLEDGMENTS

We so often believe writing must be a difficult and back-breaking endeavor, but bringing this book into being and onto the bookshelves has been an enjoyable and pain-free process. I owe this mostly to my editor, Kevin L. Lewis, who truly understood my vision; to the good people at Simon & Schuster, including Dorothy Gribbin and Joanna Feliz; and to my agent, Ethan Ellenberg, whose kind support, commitment, and brilliance got the book into the right hands. I am also deeply grateful for the wisdom of Patricia Benesh from Author Assist, without whose help the book might still be a rambling, pathetic attempt at a memoir.

Many thanks to my writing teachers over the years, especially Ehud Havazelet, Chang-Rae Lee, and Jessica Treadway, and to my twelfth-grade English teacher Harriet Falk, who first saw the writer in me. For their love, inspiration, and support, and for always challenging me to live an authentic life, I thank my dear friends, in particular Terri Brooks-Hernandez, Bevin Cahill, and Kristin Rotas. I am also indebted to my parents, Nancy Church and Kenneth Cohen, for their enduring support, and to Tyler Cohen, who has always been my biggest fan.

I am thankful to the writing gods, who allowed me to transform something difficult and tumultuous in my life into something meaningful and, I sincerely hope, helpful to others who have taken similar paths.

And, last here, but first in my life, I am filled with gratitude for whatever forces brought Michael, Ezra, and Griffin into my life. I'll never want for male attention again.

Slut?

CHAPTER 1

It's two years ago, and I'm just about to turn twelve. At home things are just about to turn too. My mother spends most of her time crying in the bedroom or the kitchen, or wherever someone might hear. To get away, I'm in the woods near the house. Wandering. Suddenly he's there, walking toward me. His face blank. His breathing ragged, audible. I've seen him before. He's mentally retarded. The boy who never grew up. But he's different this time. There's something distant in his eyes, and strange. As he comes closer, I see why—his fly is open and from it stands his erect penis. It's pale and fishlike, an alien thing. I take a step backward. He stares at me and says nothing. I turn and run—

Screeching brakes from a semitruck bring me back. I'm on one of my walks, waiting to cross the busy freeway. The driver is watching me and blasts the horn. He's maybe

1

thirty years old, wearing a white tank top. He has blond hair and thick stubble. His window is rolled all the way down and his arm rests on the top. He sits up high, but he's close enough for me to see the sun glinting off the pale, short hairs on his arm. My eyes lock on his and he flashes a warm, friendly grin. There is something else in his eyes too. He's interested, admiring.

My body fills with warmth, as though heat is seeping from the sidewalk through my flip-flops all the way to my face. I like the feeling, his eyes lingering on my small new breasts. I smile back. I reach into my pocket for my camera.

"Hey, there," he says. Before I can take a picture, the brakes of the truck release, the gears shift, and he is gone. I watch after him, wanting something, wishing there were more. Wondering if his erect penis looks pale and fishlike.

When I get back to my house, my sister Anne is sweeping the kitchen floor.

"Hey," I say. I want to tell her about the man in the truck, but what would I say? She pauses a moment, looks at me, and pushes her glasses up the bridge of her nose. She's only two years older than I am, but sometimes she's like a middle-aged woman.

"Where have you been, Jessica?" Mom is at the sink, sponging a counter. Her arm moves in quick jabs. She turns to frown at me. It's Dad's weekend with Anne and me, so Mom is starting her regular meltdown. Even though they divorced almost a year ago, she won't forgive Dad for the affair.

"I took a walk," I say.

"You wanted that expensive photography class, and then you don't show up."

Oops. I forgot.

When I signed up for the four-week class in June, it was all I could think about. I couldn't wait for the class to start. Mom turns around again so I can see only her petite back and dark hair. She is a bundle of darkness.

"Who do you think I am? Your personal chauffeur? I'm supposed to wait for you? I have a life too," she says.

I set my mouth so I won't blurt out anything. Mom misunderstands whatever I say. I go up to my room. The contest information sits on my desk. Ruth's handwriting is at the top: DON'T FORGET! She's been my art teacher since seventh grade. The big blue letters seem to mock me. "Forget" is my new middle name. Ruth's in charge at our school of this year's national high school art contest. The prize is five thousand dollars and a chance to show your work in the National Gallery in Washington, D.C., where thousands of people will see it. This is the first year I'll be able to submit my work. I just started my first year in high school.

"You have a gift," Ruth told me once while sifting

through photos I had just developed in the darkroom. I've held on to that idea ever since: a gift, waiting to be unwrapped. I want more than anything to win that prize. And not for the money. For the chance to be seen.

The deadline is December fifteenth, three months away. The theme of this year's contest is self-portrait. Last year it was nature. That sounds much easier.

I take my digital Canon out of my pocket, place it carefully on the desk, and pick up the manual Canon that Dad bought for my twelfth birthday. I stand in front of the floor-length mirror. Other than my long light hair and the mole on my jaw, I barely recognize myself. My hips are wide, my breasts swollen. I have three zits on my forehead. Even my feet seem strange and not mine.

How will I take a self-portrait if I don't know who I am anymore? I hold up the camera, adjust the focus, and *snap!* I don't know what the picture will look like, but sometimes my camera sees better than I do.

I hear a horn honking outside. It's Dad in his white Mustang. I come downstairs just in time to see Mom running to her room without saying good-bye. I catch Anne looking back at the stairs twice before she closes the door behind us. Anne and I hump our backpacks out to the car. It is late afternoon, almost evening. My favorite time of day, when the sky seems to lift and the sun shoots out at an angle, no longer right overhead and punishing. All the photos I take in this light come out tinted blue.

"There's my girls," Dad says. He's leaning against the passenger door, his smile big, his light hair flapping a bit in the breeze. He reaches out to take our packs, and, though Anne lets him take her bag, she shrinks away from him when he goes to hug her. I let him hug me, though. He rustles my hair, which is the same color as his. Then he looks me up and down. I cross my arms over my chest, not wanting him to see my breasts.

"Every time I see you girls lately, you look so different that you'd think I hadn't seen you in years." He says it cheerfully, but when I look at his face, I can see that he's sad. I wait for him to say something about the sadness, but he just smiles and opens the car door for me. Anne avoids his eyes, but I smile back, knowing it's what he wants—his girls should be cheerful too.

"Can we have Friendly's tonight?" I ask as soon as we're all in the car.

Anne's in the front seat. I'm in the back. Dad looks over at Anne, whose gaze is fixed out the window. "What do you think, Anne?"

Anne shrugs. "Whatever."

I press my fingers into the vinyl seat, trying to think of something good to say, something that will take Dad's mind off Anne's attitude. "Let's go to the one near the mini-golf course."

"Sounds like a plan," Dad says. Then, "We just have to make one stop."

My stomach drops. "I knew it," Anne says.

"You just have to get to know her," Dad says. His voice is pleading. "Dana's really great."

"I'm sure," Anne says. She still won't look at him.

"I thought it was just going to be us this weekend," I say. It has been every other weekend, just Dad and Anne and me.

"Well," Dad says, "starting this weekend things are going to be different."

After dinner we walk into Dad's apartment. It's strange to see all his things, all the stuff he bought when he moved in. I pull my digital out of my pocket and eye the room through the screen. A one-bedroom with a foldout futon for a couch. A TV. A desk with Dad's computer. A kitchen table with four metal-legged chairs.

Dana shows up in the screen. I follow her with the lens. She walks into the kitchen, opens a cabinet, and pulls out a glass, knowing where everything is. She flips her blond hair over a shoulder and turns on the tap to fill her glass. She is comfortable here.

Dad enters the screen. He comes up beside Dana, puts a hand on the small of her back, just above her butt. He knows where everything is too. I glance over at Anne to see if she's watching, but she is already sitting on the futon, her bag on her lap, putting on her I-hate-being-here-so-let's-just-get-this-over-with look. She didn't say one word during dinner.

That night Anne and I lie on the futon. The mattress is hard. Shadows of leaves jump across the ceiling, making pretty shapes. I can hear the hum of cars on the street. It is always hard to fall asleep the first night here. Especially tonight, knowing Dana is here in the bedroom with Dad. Knowing they are together, under the covers. I focus on Anne's breathing, hoping the pulse of her breath will quiet my mind, but I can tell by the quickness that she is awake too.

Instead I think about boys. It is what I do lately when I can't sleep: I pick a boy—one I know, one I saw, or one I made up—and I imagine how things might go. Tonight I imagine there is a new boy in the ninth grade. He has dark shaggy hair hanging into his eyes, and he wears ruined jeans low on his hips. He doesn't know his way around yet, so he asks me where algebra class is. Wouldn't you know it? We have algebra together. After school we get on the same bus because, it turns out, he just moved into a house on my street. After the bus drops us off, we walk together and talk about everything. Then, in front of my house, he leans forward and kisses me. Soon his hands are in my hair and on my back. "You're what I've been waiting for," he whispers, and he presses his warm body against mine. His hands work their way down my back to my behind, and he pulls me into him—Just then a noise breaks into my fantasy, a sound I don't quite recognize.

I listen. It's Dana, making noises with my father, on the other side of the wall. My stomach goes hollow and the blood rushes into my face. Worse, I can feel a tingle between my legs, sent there by my fantasy boy, but egged on by Dana's moans. I slide my hands up slowly to cover my ears, hoping I don't wake Anne. Anne rolls away from me. She hears it too.

CHAPTER 2

No, she didn't," Elisabeth says. We are at the movie theater, waiting in line for popcorn. Elisabeth stares at me with big brown eyes, her dark bobbed hair swinging as she shakes her head.

"Oh, yes she did," I say. I am telling her about last night, about Dana, and my Dad.

"You must have felt so ashamed." Shame is Elisabeth's new subject. She discusses it whenever possible. She's interested in pop-psychology. She has been ever since her father died seven years ago, leaving her and her mother alone. I guess it helps her make sense of things. I start to respond, something about her working shame into the conversation, when I see him. Jason. The boy I would kill for. The boy I have been wagging my tongue at since fourth grade when he first moved to New Jersey and showed up in Mrs. Kennedy's homeroom. Elisabeth follows my eyes. "Oh, no," she says.

"Oh, yes." Jason laughs at something his friend Shane says as he hands his ticket to the kid waiting. His eyes, which I already know are a deep shade of brown, sparkle. Jason looks like a dirty blond Ethan Hawke. He is the most beautiful boy I have ever seen, including Brad Pitt and Leo DiCaprio. He and Shane walk toward the popcorn line. I love the way he walks, the way he drags his feet as though he is in no hurry to get anywhere. His eyes pass over mine, then come back. I smile. So does he.

"Could we just get our popcorn and find a seat?" Elisabeth asks, annoyed.

"I'm just going to say hello." I leave Elisabeth standing there and make my way over to Jason. He isn't looking, but when I say hi, he turns to face me and I watch as his eyes glance quickly up and down my body. I know he sees me, my new hips, my breasts. I press out my chest just slightly. "Which movie are you seeing?"

"*Extreme Terror*," he tells me. I can't tell whether he wants to talk to me. Shane is watching me, so I smile at him, too. It can't hurt to have his friends think I'm cute.

"Hey," I say. Shane nods. "That's what we're seeing too," I lie. "Maybe we'll see you in there."

"Sure," Jason says. I head back over to Elisabeth, who cuts her eyes at me.

"You owe me four bucks," she says. She's holding the large popcorn and a Coke. With her body still skinny and undeveloped, she looks like a little girl standing there. I feel bad, making her wait.

"Listen," I say, "would it be okay if we saw *Extreme Terror* instead?"

Elisabeth's face grows red and blotchy like it always does when she's upset. "You go," she says. "I'm going to see the movie we agreed to."

"Okay," I say. "Forget it. It was just an idea." I look up and see Jason and Shane ordering popcorn. I pull out my pocket Canon and sneak a few photos of Jason. I can look at them later, when Elisabeth's not around.

On Monday I go to the darkroom to see how my self-portrait came out. I dip the contact print in the hypo, then the stop bath, and hang it by clothespins and wait. Ruth and I have an arrangement that I can work in the darkroom after school. She gives me extra credit for it. I've always liked the way the rest of the world goes away in here, how the universe becomes just this: me and my photographs. Slowly the picture comes into being. First it is just a shadowy ghost, then an outline, and finally I sharpen and step into the room. I am just jeans and a face with a camera. The rest of me is washed

11

out, hidden behind the bright light of the flash. The picture is interesting but says nothing. I yank it down, ripping the edge, and crumple it into a ball. As I emerge from the darkroom and into the hallway, Ruth sees me. She puts her hands on my shoulders. Ruth has always been affectionate with students. Her salt-and-pepper hair is held back with two combs, and she's wearing one of her hippie skirts. Students call her Tie-Dye behind her back, but I feel protective of her. She's always been nice to me.

"Any ideas yet?" she asks me.

"Sure," I lie. A few students pass by. They look over to see what's going on. "I'm working on a few things."

Ruth's eyes are soft and pouchy. She never wears make-up. She should. She has the potential to be pretty. "I know you'll come up with something great." She smiles and releases me. I feel awful. I'm a failure. I have nothing. No ideas. No pictures. I head toward the cafeteria for lunch.

Ashley, Shane's girlfriend and the most popular girl in the ninth grade, passes with a group of her friends. She says hello. If she were to turn a camera on me right now, what would she see through the lens? An average girl. Nothing special, except I can take good pictures. Or, I used to take good pictures. And without it I am back to average, blended in with the background. Without it I barely exist.

In the cafeteria the first person I see is Tiffany, sitting

by herself, of course. Ever since she developed breasts in the fourth grade, way before everybody else, she has been sitting alone. She is, officially, our school slut. Before, she and I were friends. Every so often we played together at each other's houses. We colored in books or played board games. Once people ostracized her, though, I kept my distance. I didn't want to be mean, but I had to do what I had to do.

Next I see Jason. He sits with Shane, Josh, and Ry at the table nearest the lunch line. It's where he sat in eighth grade and seventh grade, too. I'll bet he never questions whether he matters. He just knows he does. His friends are laughing at something he has said, and as I watch, Jason glances up at me. I should look away. I shouldn't be so obvious. But I can't help it. I am trapped in his eyes. Those gorgeous brown eyes. And then a half smile creeps onto his face. It is not a nice smile. It's something else. Something we share, just he and I. Like he knows the ways I've thought about him late at night, when I can't sleep. I can feel my face grow warm, and I turn away, ashamed, as Elisabeth would say. I get in the lunch line, but I can't shake the feeling Jason gave me. And I like it much better than worrying about the contest.

After school I take a walk. The air smells of dried leaves. Everywhere is orange and rust and yellow. Colors I can never capture with my camera. I try anyway. I take the Canon from my book bag, focus, and *snap!* You never know when you've taken the perfect shot. A billboard shows a woman's body reclining. She wears a shiny red negligee, a suggestive smile, and a milk mustache. MILK DOES A BODY GOOD, it says across the bottom. Beneath the billboard is a bus stop where a girl with ripped lace stockings stands and talks on her cell phone. Sitting beside her is an old man with a cane. A photo opportunity. *Snap!*

I put my camera away to focus on the cars speeding by. Or, rather, to focus on who might be in the cars. Sure enough, a man slows down to take a look. I swing my hips, lift my eyes just slightly, and smile. He hoots as he passes. Another one whistles. I know this is stupid, inviting trouble. But it feels so good to be wanted, I can't help myself. A man in a silver Honda Civic slows down to look. Next thing I know, he's on the shoulder. I keep walking, afraid to look. Afraid of what I've done. Finally things have gone too far. I can hear his window rolling down.

"You look lost," he calls to me.

I turn to see. He's a young guy, attractive even. He has dark long hair pulled into a ponytail, and dark eyes. He wears a beat-up T-shirt.

"I'm not," I tell him.

I watch as his eyes move up and down my body. My instinct is to cross my arms over my chest, but I like it from this guy. His eyes are pretty, with dark long lashes like a girl's.

"Then what are you doing here?" he asks me. "This is a busy freeway. It's no place for a little girl to take a walk."

"I'm not a little girl."

"Really?" He smiles, revealing a gap between his two front teeth. "How old are you?"

"None of your business," I tell him. I move a little closer.

"You can't be eighteen," he says, as though finishing a conversation in his mind.

"What if I am?"

He laughs. "If you are, I'm taking you home with me."

I laugh too, but I stay where I am.

"Come on," he says. "Hop in."

My heart pounds. I can feel sweat gathering at my armpits. "I don't think so."

"Why not?"

"I can't," I say. "Not now."

"Okay," he says. "Another time then." He winks. He turns on his signal and pulls back onto the street. I watch his car get smaller, then disappear around the bend. Instead of relief I feel disappointed, like I've just missed out on something big. My chance to matter.

CHAPTER 3

When I walk in the front door, I hear familiar chatter from the living room. Once a month Mom hosts a women's book group she started. She's an English teacher at a high school a few towns away, and, even more than reading them, she loves talking about books. I peer around the corner of the foyer to see eight women sitting on our couch, chairs, and pillows on the floor. Anne is there too, perched on the easy chair. Mom looks up.

"You all know my other daughter, Jessica," she says brightly. She extends her arm to me, inviting me to come. She is like a different person when people are watching her.

The women smile, pausing from their tea and coffee. Most have pieces of pound cake on napkins balancing on their knees. A few look me up and down, disapproving

17

probably of my tight jeans and skimpy shirt. I recognize one woman as Tiffany's mother. She has platinum hair and heavy makeup. I remember from when Tiffany and I were friends that all her furniture was white.

"I have homework," I tell Mom.

Mom's smile is tight and unmoving. "You can say hello for a moment," she says. I bite my lip and move closer, letting Mom slide her arm around my waist. Anne flips through the book on her lap. She's the only one, I notice, who is actually holding a book.

"What are you reading?" I ask. I know Mom will appreciate my showing interest. At the least she will let me go upstairs sooner.

"*The Poisonwood Bible*," one of the women says. She has frizzy hair and glasses too big for her face. "Have you read it?"

I shake my head. Unlike Anne, I'm not much of a reader.

"I only read when I have to," I say.

Mom leans forward, releasing me. That same smile is stuck on her face. "I don't know where she came from," she says. "Anne and I are such avid readers."

Anne glances at me quickly, then looks back at the book. I watch my sneaker as I move it back and forth on the carpet, not wanting to see anyone else's expression. Maybe she doesn't know what she sounds like when she says stuff like that.

"Some people like to read, and others don't," a woman says. "We're all different."

The room is quiet.

"I do photography," I say after a few moments, to defend myself.

The room erupts in oh's and ah's. They seem eager to break the discomfort.

"Should we get back to discussing Leah's character?" Mom says when the room settles. With that, I slip out.

Elisabeth passes me the plate of cookies. She can eat anything and stay skinny as a pole. Ever since my body changed, a cookie goes straight to my thighs, just like Mom. I take one anyway, thinking I won't eat more. We are sitting on Elisabeth's bed. One of the Olsen twins smiles from the shiny cover of the *Seventeen* between us. The walls are pink. Dolls line an upper shelf. She hasn't changed her room since we met, back in the second grade. That was right after her father died from cancer and she and her mother moved to New Jersey to be closer to family. I'd suggest she redecorate, but she only repositions one of the dolls or changes its outfit. She's still comfortable in her childhood room. Maybe it helps her stay close to her father's memory.

"Coach thinks we can go to state," she says. She's talking about track. She has cross-country, I have photography.

It's always been like that. During recess in second grade she ran and ran around the playground while David Shafer chased her. I wandered off near the trees, examining the way the sunlight shifted on the leaves. I didn't care back then whether a boy looked at me or not. Now I can barely keep my own eyes still long enough to focus the camera. She can tell I'm distracted. "How's the contest coming?"

"Ugh," I say. "Don't remind me."

"I'm sure you'll think of something."

"Why does everyone keep saying that?"

Elisabeth gets up and pulls open her blinds. Her back is facing me.

"I'm sorry, Lizzie," I say. "I just don't want to talk about it."

She looks back at me and pushes a strand of hair behind her ear. "Then what *do* you want to talk about? Let me guess: Jason."

"What's gotten into you?"

"Me?" she says. "You're the one who's changed."

I look down at my hands. There's a smudge of chocolate on my thumb from the cookie. I know she's right. What would she say if she knew about my walks? If she knew about the guy in the Civic, how I've thought of him ever since? She would probably be appalled. "Let's just talk," I say. "What do you want to talk about?"

Right then Elisabeth's mother knocks on the door.

"Come in," Elisabeth calls without hesitation. This is another way we are nothing alike. She is exceptionally close to her mother, who she refers to by first name. She calls Deb her other best friend. And, from the way Elisabeth talks about her, she can do no wrong. Elisabeth's the one interested in psychology, so I'm amazed she hasn't figured out *why* she has to be best friends with her mother. Who else does she have?

"How are we doing on cookies?" Deb asks. Her dark hair falls loosely over her shoulders, and she is thin like Elisabeth. They look like sisters.

"We're good," Elisabeth says. She gives Deb a look that says she'll talk to her later. Deb nods and closes the door. We're silent a moment.

I breathe in, trying to come up with the right thing to say. "You're so lucky," I say once Deb closes the door. "Your mom is so great."

Elisabeth smiles and moves back toward the bed. She likes it when I compliment her mother. I mean it, though. Deb has always been kind to me. But I know saying so will get me back in Elisabeth's good graces.

"She's the best," she says.

"Lizzie." I scrunch my face. "I'm sorry I've been such an ass."

Elisabeth looks at me. "A double ass," she says.

"Triple," I say.

21

She laughs.

I breathe out and laugh with her. We're back to normal.

At home the house is quiet and dark. When I go upstairs, I can hear my mother's muffled sobs through Anne's bedroom door.

"Who would have me?" my mother says. "I'm used and old."

"No," Anne says quietly.

"Your father left me. Who will ever love me again?"

"I do," Anne says. "I love you."

I tiptoe away from the door, not wanting them to hear me. Not wanting to hear them.

In my room I pull down my book of twentieth-century photography. Why is there no chapter on self-portraits? Most photographers, it seems, avoided the subject. I understand why. They focused on what was outside them: people, shadows, shapes. The same things I like to focus on. On my wall are the ones I'm most proud of, including the shot of the circular stairwell that won first prize in the Bergen Country Day eighth-grade art contest. I wasn't up against high school kids all over the country then. Leafing through the book, I stop on Cindy Sherman. Almost all her work is self-portraits. Here she is a man. Here she is dressed in lace. Here she is a corpse. She is brilliant, sliding into various identities. She tells who she is by becoming a tiny piece of who she is and who she is not. I wish I could be as clear.

I pull down shoe boxes from the top shelf of my closet. I sift through the photographs. Elisabeth and me in Manhattan. Dad and Anne and me. Mom and Dad with us when we were little. Dad hangs his arm loosely over Mom's shoulder. They look comfortable, settled. Mom told me they got pregnant with Anne a month after being married. They were anxious to have a family, and they were very much in love. They assumed, as I guess all married couples do, that their feelings would last forever. They didn't count on job and kid stresses. They didn't count on Dad pulling away and Mom grasping tighter, desperate for her life to be what she had planned. In the photograph they stare out at me, serene and unknowing. It's hard to understand these are the same people, now as frantic and restless as wild animals.

I hear Anne's door open, then click shut. I hear Mom pad toward her bedroom. I stay perfectly still, hoping she won't hear me. But she stops outside my door, probably seeing my light.

"Jessica?" she asks.

"What."

"You're home."

I watch the door, willing it to not open. She knows I won't let her cry to me the way she does with Anne, but I have to keep my shield up to make sure. If I let it down for even a second, she might forget.

"Well, okay," Mom says when I don't respond. "Good night."

I listen for her door to close, then I crumple the photo of our family and throw it at the wastebasket. It misses, hits the wall, and rolls under my desk out of sight.

I'm in the darkroom, where everything is still. The red light makes me feel as though I am in another dimension, like being underwater, the world dreamlike and illuminated. First I dip the pictures from the freeway. The leaves one is unremarkable, but I like the photograph of the girl on the phone. I can feel her sharp energy, almost angry, next to the old man. Why can't the contest be about other people?

Next I dip the prints of Jason and watch him come into being. I can see the slump of his shoulders and the way he rests his weight to one side. I can see the light in his hair, the roundness of his lips. Just looking at his picture makes me buzz with a want I can feel all the way down to my toes. The desire is so strong I feel like I'm going to explode or scream or melt away. I've never felt like this before, like a dam about to burst. It's scary, but exciting. Like something's got to happen.

There's a knock and, without waiting for an answer, Ruth slips into the room. I don't have time to pull my Jason pictures down, so she sees them. Sees me looking at them.

"I thought I'd check in on you," she says, looking at the pictures as I start undoing the clothespins. "What are these?"

"Just some photos," I say. "I was playing around."

She nods, watching me with a smile on her face. I don't meet her eyes, just keep taking down my pictures.

"I was hoping I'd catch you with something you were working on for the contest."

I don't say anything. I wave the photos in the air, hoping they're dry enough, and stuff them into my book bag.

"Was that Jason Reilly?" she asks.

I nod.

Her smile increases. "Are you two together?"

"No," I say. "Not really." I glance at the door, wondering how to escape. I don't want to talk to Ruth about this. She's known me for three years now, since I was eleven, since I thought boys were annoying, when I used to say the only thing that mattered in the world was my photography. I'm too embarrassed to have her know how mundane and pathetic I've become.

"You'd make a cute couple."

I reach for my bag. "I've got to go," I say, and I bolt out of there. But sitting on the late bus home, I can't help but smile at the idea that Jason and I would make a cute couple. Mom stares straight ahead, gripping the steering wheel of our old minivan. She drives like an old woman, slow and full of anxiety. At this rate I'll never get to the photography class on time.

"I hope you're planning on spending the weekend with Anne and me," Mom says.

"Fine," I say.

"With you two gone at your father's so much," she says, "I don't get any help."

I hold my manual Canon on my lap and look out the window at the passing buildings. I want Mom to be happy, but why does it always seem to be at my own expense?

"Are you even listening to me?" she says.

"I said fine."

"You don't have to keep it a secret," she says after a moment.

I look at her, my pulse quickening. I think about my walks, about the guy in the Civic. I wonder how she could know.

"A secret?" I ask. Her dark hair is pulled back, and I can see the tiny lines around her eyes. They call them laugh lines, but I can't remember the last time I saw her laugh. I wait, squeezing my camera.

"You can tell me about that woman he's with." Her face stays hard and unmoving. It takes me a second, but then I realize she's talking about Dana.

"Mom," I say.

"No," she says. "I'd rather you tell me than have everyone hide it from me."

"Nobody's hiding anything."

"I'm not some fool, you know," she says. This time her voice breaks and tears spring into her eyes. I look back out the window. A young woman is running with her dog on the sidewalk. I watch her running and running until she turns a corner, out of view. Mom slows down in front of the community college art building, where the class is taking place.

"I'm going to be late," I say, and I jet out the door without looking back.

As I approach the entrance to the building, I can already see this is a mistake. Three college-aged women are talking and smoking cigarettes, their fancy, expensive cameras over their shoulders. My camera is nice, but it's not top of the line like those. A white-haired man who must be the teacher walks past them and waves hello. He holds a tripod and a box meant for contact sheets. I watch as another man trots to catch up with him. He says something to the teacher, and they laugh. They all know each other already, having been together last week.

I duck behind a tree. After a minute they all disappear inside. That's when I head back to the road. It's a long walk home, plus I don't want Mom to know I didn't go to the class. I consider calling Dad, but he's probably out with

Dana or, worse, in bed with Dana. So I go across the street to Starbucks. I figure I'll wait there until it's time to call Mom to pick me up.

I get a latte and sit outside, facing the street. The air is cool. We're one week into October, and already the leaves are filling the streets. Cars pass, and I find myself looking for the silver Civic. He would surely stop, wondering what I was doing here, all by myself. He would listen as I talked about my mother, and he would hold me while I talked about the ways in which I felt so alone. Cars pass, none of them him. Right then I decide I will go with him if I ever get the chance again.

CHAPTER 4

I take a walk, timing it so I'm there right at the same time. Sure enough, a silver Civic comes around the bend, then slows onto the shoulder.

"Hey," he says, smiling. His eyes twinkle.

"Hey," I say. This time I'm not walking away. I move around to the passenger side and open the door. Inside it smells like car freshener and French fries and something musky I don't recognize. I push a crumpled McDonald's bag aside with my foot. I'm wearing the black high-heeled boots I wore for Halloween last year, when I was Catwoman. And a short black skirt that I'm regretting. He reaches down to grab the bag, brushing my leg as he does, and he throws the bag into the backseat. I glance back to see a tremendous pile of fast-food bags and empty soda bottles. I also see a car magazine jutting out beneath a bag—a woman's leg on top of the hood of a car. Heat creeps up my body. So does the realization he could be a serial killer or a rapist. This could be the stupidest thing I've ever done. He smiles at me.

"I haven't cleaned it out in a while." This close I can see stubble on his chin. He moves the gearshift, his forearm tensing. There's a spattering of freckles beneath the hair. I don't say anything, my heart banging at my chest like a drum. I keep my eyes on my legs, which look fat spread out on the vinyl seats. He watches me for a long minute.

"Hey," he says. "Don't be nervous. We're just getting something to eat."

I still can't look at him.

"Or we can do something else," he says. "Whatever you want."

"I'm not hungry," I tell him.

"Okay," he says. When I still don't say anything, he places a gentle finger beneath my chin. On his hand I smell the scent I can't recognize. It's him, his particular scent. He turns my face toward his. His eyes are beautiful and kind. I take a breath, and he smiles. I smile back. "How about ice cream?" he asks, and I nod.

At the ice cream parlor he steps out of his car. He is shorter than I had imagined, but he is still attractive. His name is Ted. He's twenty years old.

We walk inside. With my two-inch heels, I am almost as tall as he is. I can feel his eyes on my body. I consider what an eighteen-year-old would order and decide on mint chocolate chip in a dish. He gets a double chocolate cone. We sit at a table by the door, even though anyone from school could walk by. Elisabeth could come in with her mother. Dad and Dana could come in. How do I know what they do when they're not having sex? Amazingly, no one I know comes through the door.

An hour later we're sitting in the Civic a few houses down from mine. I tell him the big brick one is my house. The Gibbonses live there with their twin baby boys. I babysat for them a couple times over the summer. While I consider saying something about my baby brothers, just in case they come out of the house, Ted leans in and kisses me. It takes me by surprise, my first kiss. Warm and wet. I can feel his stubble on my cheek. His tongue darts into my mouth. A jolt of energy runs from my mouth down to my legs. When he leans back, I put my hand up to my mouth.

"I'm glad you were there today," he says.

"Me too," I tell him.

"I've been back there every day looking for you."

"You have?"

"I couldn't help myself," he says. "Look at you. You're irresistible."

Nobody's ever said anything like this to me before. I smile, unsure what to say.

"When can I see you again?"

The sky is darkening, turning to evening. I have homework to finish and school tomorrow. And then there's the contest, for which I still have nothing. "I don't know," I tell him.

He frowns. "Come on," he says. "Give me your number."

"How about you give me yours?" I say, knowing I have to keep Ted a secret at home.

"If you aren't interested, just say so," he says in a low voice. "I don't want to play games."

"Really," I say, thinking fast. "We're having some trouble with the phone company. Our number's not working."

He watches me, trying to gauge whether to believe me. Finally he gently takes my hand and turns it over. He pulls a pen from his dash and writes his number across my palm. I close the door and walk toward the Gibbonses' front door, until he takes off. Then I head home, my fingers closed in a fist over his number.

At home there are two messages: one from Elisabeth and one from Dad. Elisabeth wants to tell me about practice. Dad says he expects to be a couple hours late to get us on Friday. He doesn't say so, but it has Dana written all over it.

I look up at the mirror in the front foyer. I put my fingers to my mouth. I've been kissed. These lips have been kissed. Elisabeth would freak if I told her. But I can't.

"Mom's out." I turn around to see Anne. My hand drops from my face, and I close it so she can't see the number written on the palm.

"So?"

"She had a date." She waits. When I don't say anything, she says, "I'm supposed to make us dinner."

"I'm not hungry," I say. I head for my room. Anne just stands there. She's been waiting here, I guess, for someone to come home. Since the divorce she's spent all her time with Mom. I stop at the stairs, guilty. "What are you making?"

"Macaroni and cheese." Her short dark hair hangs flat against her face. If I glanced quickly at her, she could almost be Mom.

I move off the stairs, my hand still in a fist.

"Who's Mom dating?" I ask with a grimace.

Anne looks pained. She pushes her hair behind her ear. "She met him at the grocery store. He told her she looked like Judy Garland."

I wait. Anne obviously has something to say about it. "She thinks that means something," Anne says.

"Maybe it does," I say. "Why not be happy for her?"

"She needs someone who will love her for her, not for how she looks."

33

Like you're the expert on love, I want to say. I know how good it can feel to have a man tell you something nice, like when Ted told me I was irresistible. Instead I say, "Why don't you focus on what you need and let Mom focus on what she needs?"

Anne walks away, her brow furrowed. But I'm happy for Mom. Dad was cheating on her for three years before he announced his plans to leave. Surely she knew but didn't want to accept the truth. Surely that cut away at her self-esteem, knowing he was choosing another woman over her. Maybe Anne's wrong. Maybe having a man tell her she looks like a beautiful star is exactly what she needs.

That night, though, when I'm already in bed, I hear Mom come home, then the click of the door as she goes into Anne's room. Soon after, I hear her sobs as they float through the door, and I pull the pillow down over my head.

"Where were you yesterday?" Elisabeth wants to know. We're in biology class, but Mr. Landon is so old he can hear us only when we talk really loud. That can be a pain, but it works well when we just want to chat.

"I was holed up in my room," I lie. "Working on some things for the contest." Which is what I should have been doing.

"Anything?"

I shake my head. Two seats forward and one to the left

sits Jason. He has a blue cap on. His leg stretches into the aisle and bounces slightly. I know someone else has just kissed me, but Jason trumps Ted every time. I slip my digital out of my pocket and zoom in on the back of Jason's neck, which is visible through the wisps of blond hair sticking out beneath his cap. Elisabeth leans over and looks into the screen.

"He moves through girls like they're potato chips," she says.

"I know," I say defensively.

"He can have anyone he wants."

"I get it," I say. "So why would he want me?" I watch as he points his toe in and out, in and out.

"I just don't want you getting hurt."

"Lizzie," I say, "you don't have to worry about me."

I can feel her staring at me.

"He'll be at Ashley's party," she says.

"I know." I've already picked out my outfit: the black miniskirt and a ripped concert tee.

Jason turns his head as though sensing my camera's gaze. Heat comes into my face when he smiles in the screen. I snap a picture before he can look away.

Ruth once told me a photograph can capture the truth, but only if the photographer is willing to see it first. I think of this now as I position my manual Canon and set the timer.

Am I willing to see who I am? I stand before the camera, my arms at my sides, my gaze level with the lens. I wait for the *snap!* Then I set the timer again. I am determined to fill a whole roll of 35 millimeter if that's what it takes. I go back and forth, standing, sitting, kneeling, hands beside me, behind me, underneath my chin. I am single-minded in getting to the right picture, in capturing the truth.

Three-quarters through the roll something catches my eye out the window. It is a silver Civic, idling in front of the Gibbonses' house. Oh, God. I throw on a hoodie, tie my hair back, and apply some eyeliner so I look closer to eighteen. I race out the back door and, hiding behind bushes, get myself into the Gibbonses' backyard. Then I saunter up to the Civic.

"What are you doing?" I ask.

He smiles. "What do you think I'm doing?" He leans to the passenger side and opens the door.

I stay still, my heart beating quickly from running over here. I glance back at the Gibbonses' house, hoping no one is looking out a window. "You can't just sit here like this," I tell him.

"You didn't call me." He's wearing sunglasses. It's obvious he isn't going anywhere, so I go around to the passenger side and get in.

"Drive," I say.

He moves toward me. "One kiss," he says, "and I'll do whatever you want."

Our lips meet. I pull back, not wanting anyone to see, but his mouth is insistent. He presses his tongue into my mouth.

"I can't stay long," I say once he's pulled the car off my street.

I watch as his jaw muscle jumps. "Why are you like that?" he says.

"Like what?"

"Why are you always wanting to get away from me?" He slows through a stop sign, and the car juts forward when he presses on the gas.

"That's not it," I say. I reach up to find the handle above the window. The Oh-crap! handle, Elisabeth calls it. She never uses actual swear words. "I've just got a lot going on."

"Don't you think I have stuff going on?" he says. "I work at the Shopmart all day."

"I didn't know that," I say.

"Well," he says. He shifts gears, and we slow down a bit. "I hate it. I don't want to work there my whole life."

His finger traces the Honda symbol on the steering wheel. His shoulders slump forward. I see in this brief moment that he doesn't like himself. It is something my camera might catch if I had it with me. Then the moment is gone. "I'm sorry," I say.

He shrugs. "I'm twenty years old and I have no clue

what to do with my life." He glances at me. "How sad is that?"

I bite the side of my cheek, trying to come up with something to say. "I'm sure you're not the only one," I say finally.

He puts a hand on my jeans. "I knew you weren't like other girls."

I look down at his hand, at the veins crawling beneath the skin. The warmth from his hand seeps through my jeans and creeps through my body all the way to my fingertips. Sometimes I don't like myself either. I want to tell him, but I wouldn't know how.

So I say, "Pull over." And when he does, I lean into him. This time I'm the one with the insistent mouth. I can practically feel him melting beneath me.

After a few minutes he pulls back.

"Man," he says, laughing. "What are you trying to do to me?"

When he drops me off, I tell him to meet me at the community college on Friday, right in time for my class. Then I navigate my way through the backyards, my body still buzzing.

CHAPTER 5

Five boys sitting on the floor check out my legs when Elisabeth and I walk in. A DJ with headphones is bouncing to the beat. Leave it to Ashley to hire a DJ. A mass of Ashley's friends huddle together, half-dancing, half-laughing. It smells of shampoo and pot. Shane and Ashley have their arms around each other. His hand sits on her behind. A girl I only sort of know hands me a beer, and I thank her. I take my first swig.

In the far corner, laughing with Ry, stands Jason.

"You look awesome," a girl from art class wearing pigtails says. "You should dress like that more often."

"Thanks," I say. I left Dad's wearing jeans, which are now stuffed inside my purse. I didn't want to chance an argument about it. Not tonight. I keep one eye on Jason.

"Are you submitting for the contest this year?" she asks.

"Maybe," I say.

"But aren't you, like, Ruth's pride and joy?"

I shrug. She's starting to annoy me.

"I'm not," I say when she rolls her eyes.

"You should be proud," she says. "It means you're good at art."

"Whatever," I say. But the truth is she's hit my panic button. Only two more months until the deadline. I take another swig and look for Jason, who's slipped out of sight.

A few hours and two beers later, though, we almost crash into each other.

"Hey, camera girl," he says. He's drunk. "Can I call you that?"

"You can call me whatever you want," I whisper in his ear. I'm a little drunk myself.

Jason takes me by the hand. He pulls me through the crowd and up the stairs. I am all hands. I am all *that* hand. The one Jason's holding. The one Jason Reilly is finally holding.

"Hey, camera girl," he says again, once we are behind a door. This time he says it up close, near my lips. I close my eyes and feel his warm lips as they reach mine. His hands move down my back to my waist, and then they crawl up again, under my shirt, until they find my bra. He unsnaps it: a pro, but I won't let myself think about that. Instead I focus on the smell of him: beer and laundry detergent. And the fact that it is perfectly quiet, except for the sound of our breath and the muffled beat of music in a party full of people far away.

He pulls away before I want him to, leaving me breathless, my arms itching to have him back. He smiles, but he's looking elsewhere. And, in a second, he's gone again, down the stairs, back into the party, another bottle of beer in his hand. He's laughing with Ry. He doesn't notice when I come back to the party, my bra re-snapped, my feet three inches off the ground, and my lips tingling.

In the taxi on the way back to Dad's apartment, Elisabeth stares out the window. I know she's mad. I, on the other hand, am euphoric. Our friendship, actually, is getting to be a real drag. Finally she looks at me.

"I can't believe you," she says.

"Is it so hard to believe that Jason might really like me?"

"Yes," she says. "Because he's a bona fide jerk."

"You don't know him," I tell her.

"And you do?"

"I'm getting to know him," I say. I think of his scent, and a wave of joy passes through my throat. "You wouldn't understand," I say, and as soon as I've said it, I know it was a mistake.

"Why?" she says. "Because no boy has ever been interested in me?"

I don't say anything.

"Is that what you're saying?" she asks.

I still say nothing.

"Screw you," she says. It's almost a swear word, which means we're officially in a fight. But after being kissed by Jason Reilly, I feel as if nothing can penetrate me. It's like he put an invisible shield over my body with his wandering hands. And I find that I don't care what Elisabeth thinks. I don't care one bit.

I wake the next morning to the sound of coffee grinding. I pick my head off the pillow and look around. Anne is already out of bed, nowhere to be seen. Dana is in the kitchen, without Dad. She's in sweatpants and a T-shirt, and her hair is in a ponytail. She looks barely older than me.

"Did I wake you?" she says when she sees me.

I shrug. "It's not a big deal."

"Come in here."

I glimpse the clock on the wall: 10:15.

"Where is everyone?" I ask.

"Robert and Anne are at the grocery store," she says. It takes me a moment to catch that Robert is Dad. Mom used to call him "Dad." Now she calls him "your father." Everyone else calls him Bob. Dana smiles at me. "It's just you and me."

I nod. *Let the good times begin,* I think. Another part of me frowns. *Be nice,* this part warns.

"So," I say, heeding the warning. "Where did you and Dad meet?"

Dana smiles to herself as she pours the water into the coffeemaker.

"Your dad was very romantic," she says.

My dad? I doubt that.

"He left a bouquet of daisies at my desk."

"You work with him?"

"I'm a graphic designer at Howe Advertising," she says. The same company where Dad's an ad exec.

I watch her as she pulls down two mugs from the cabinet. Graphic design means she's artistic. I guess I hadn't pegged her as creative. But then, I hadn't really pegged her as anything. I feel a little guilty since this is the first time I've asked her anything about herself.

"Robert tells me you're a photographer," she says.

"I try," I say.

She pours coffee into the mugs and holds up the cream and sugar. I nod to both. "I'd like to see some of your work," she says.

"I could do that," I say. I take the steaming mug from her.

"My real love is painting," she tells me. I lean against the counter and blow on the coffee, wanting to hear more. "I've been using oils since I was your age."

"Do you still?" I ask.

"Whenever I can." She leans against the opposite counter.

"It's hard to fit into a forty-hour week. But I make time. I have to," she says, looking at me more intensely. "You know?"

I nod. I do know. Dad and Anne burst in the door with bags of groceries. Dad sees us standing together in the kitchen.

"How nice to see two of my three favorite girls communing in my kitchen," he says, smiling. I take my mug and head back into the living room. He makes it sound as though I'm some little kid. But Dana was talking to me as her equal. Like I could understand what really matters in life. I liked it.

On Monday I see Jason near his locker. Josh, Shane, and Ashley are there too. I comb my fingers through my hair and walk by, doing my best impression of someone who is at ease with the fact that Jason Reilly kissed her, and now here he is again, ripe for the picking.

"Hey," I say.

He turns around. "Oh," he says. "Hey."

His friends are silent. The air, a second ago vibrating with possibility, goes flat and still.

"How's it going?" I ask.

Jason shrugs.

An eternity passes. Then, his lips, the lips that kissed me, say, "Is there anything else? Because we're kind of talking about something here."

"No," I say. I make a beeline for the girls' bathroom. My face is burning. I feel like I might throw up. As soon as I get there, I lean against the wall and press my forehead to it. Right at my eye level someone has written, TIFFANY DOES IT DOGGIE STYLE.

"What's the matter?"

I turn my head to see Elisabeth there. Perfect.

"I thought you weren't talking to me," I say.

"I'm talking to you if something bad has happened," she says. "I'm still your best friend. Your codependent best friend," she adds with a half smile.

I drop my hands, relieved. I do need a friend right now.

"You promise you won't say 'I told you so'?"

Elisabeth takes my hands and walks me to the sink. "Oh, no," she says. "What did that jerk-off do?"

In the mirror I look horrible. My face is red. My eyes are watery. No wonder he doesn't like me. She turns on the cold water and puts a cool, wet hand on my forehead. She always knows exactly what I need.

"He treated me like garbage." I close my eyes, focusing on Elisabeth's hands, remembering his hands. My throat aches. "I like him so much," I whisper.

Elisabeth, bless her heart, says nothing.

When I get home, I call Ted.

"Hello, gorgeous," he says.

I sit on my bed. The door is closed so Anne won't hear.

"I'm not gorgeous," I say.

"That's your opinion."

I wait, hoping he'll say more.

"I want to see you," he says.

"Meet me at the end of my street."

After we hang up, I stand before the mirror. I am not quite as horrible as I was before. I try to see what Ted sees. I try to see "gorgeous." I pull my hair up, yank a few strands down to frame my face. I turn my face to the side. I can almost see it.

Fifteen minutes later I'm in his car, and his lips are on mine, erasing Jason's.

"Let's go to my place," he whispers.

"Not yet," I say.

"Come on." He pulls me into him, kissing my neck.

"No," I say. "Not yet."

His hands wander my skin, sliding beneath my bra straps. "You're a tease," he says. I think he's making a joke, but I take it under advisement.

In the darkroom I make prints of my self-portraits and dip them in the fixing bath. I hang the photographs, all twenty-four, and wait for them to show themselves. One by one they come to light, and one by one I see I have failed again. Some look like Sears portraits. Others resemble glamour shots. All of them show a girl with nothing unique to say. More time wasted. I close my eyes, letting the world go away for a moment. I wonder what's happened, why I can't seem to take a worthwhile photo of myself. I used to not have to think, just lift my camera and snap the shutter, confident I would find whatever was worth seeing. Now I can't even find myself.

Tiffany is the only other person on the late bus. She sees me near the back when she walks on, and sits in the front row. From where I sit, I can see her profile. She has dark curly hair and a petite nose. She's kind of pretty, actually. She pulls her history book from her bag and looks down at it. The driver starts up the motor. It is quiet, and I feel sort of bad, like maybe I should say something. Maybe I should be nice to her, unlike everybody else. After all, we used to sing songs from the radio together. We vowed we'd start a band when we grew up. I imagine moving to sit next to her and telling her about my walks and Ted. I imagine telling her the things I've been holding on to, afraid to let out. Things that, if I think about them too long, make me feel nervous and out of control. Because, of all the people I know, maybe Tiffany will understand and won't squint with disgust or decide I've lost my mind. Maybe, after all Tiffany has endured, she will know what it's like to want badly for someone to love her and not know a better way to get it. I imagine this conversation all the way to her stop, when she puts her book back in the bag and steps down from the bus, unaware I've been thinking about her at all.

CHAPTER 6

Ted has his hand on my knee. We are in his car, heading for the park, where we plan to slip into the woods and get busy. This is the last Friday to hide behind bushes after Mom has dropped me off for photography class. The last Friday to walk to the Starbucks where Ted waited for me.

Even though the weather has turned cold and there's no sign of sun, the park is full of people. Kids clamber around the playground while mothers sit on benches and talk. Two girls who can't be more than eleven practice dance moves near a large oak. They both wear thongs that show above their jeans. I aim my Canon and snap a photo. A few teenage boys play basketball nearby. Dogs chase balls across the length of the lawn. Ted is unfazed. He grabs a blanket from his trunk and heads for the wooded area lining the park. I follow, the Canon in my hand.

At the first clearing he lays down the blanket and grabs me. We roll around, our legs tangled. After a while I get up and grab my camera.

"What are you doing?" Ted asks. His breath is ragged, like he's just finished running.

I aim the camera at him. Through the lens he looks small and tightly wound, like a balloon about to burst. "Smile," I tell him.

"Come on," he reaches for me, but not before I take a shot.

"I don't have any photos of you," I say. I lean away from him and take another picture. This time he grabs the camera, and I reach after it.

"You can do this later," he says. "Right now we're doing something else."

When I reach for the camera again, he sets it on the ground next to his crotch. He undoes his jeans. "Come and get it," he says with a growl.

I bite my lip. I can hear the kids in the playground yelling. He takes my hand and presses it on his skin, against his crotch, which is hard and warm. He sucks in his breath and pulls me to him. And I take his penis fully into my hand. It is not smooth like I thought it would be, but it's not rough. It's velvety soft, pulsing with energy. As I stroke it, guided by his hand, I can feel the way it grows. It responds to my hand like something alive. Ted nudges my head down, and before I know it, I am head to head with his penis.

"I don't . . . ," I start. I'm not sure how to finish the sentence.

"Please," he says. I look up and see the desperation in his eyes. He squirms, pushing himself into me. He is like an animal.

Carefully I take it into my mouth. It is no worse than kissing. I just have to keep my mouth open longer. I can still hear the kids yelling, but they seem far away. He presses my head, urging me to go faster. I do. And soon, he moans, and warmth fills my mouth. I try to pull away, but he holds my head firmly. When he finally releases me, I squeeze my eyes and swallow, willing myself not to gag.

Ted zips his jeans and stands. He reaches for the blanket, but I'm still kneeling on it.

"Let's go," he says.

I stand, wordless. As he lifts the blanket, my camera tumbles onto the pine-needle floor. I had forgotten it was there.

When I get home, Mom and Anne are sitting on the couch watching a movie.

"There you are," Mom says. She looks like she used to,

her expression airy, the darkness hardly there. Anne is snuggled against her. A bowl of popcorn sits on the coffee table.

"What," I say. "I told you I would take a cab home."

Mom looks me up and down. I run my hand through my hair, hoping she can't see what I've just done. My finger catches on a pine needle, so I keep my hand there to hide it.

"I thought you would come straight home," she says. When I don't say anything, she says, "I wanted you to watch the movie with us. Like a family, before your father comes to get you."

I look at them sitting there. A big part of me would like that, to cuddle up with Mom on the couch, like the old days. But I smell like Ted and God-knows-what-else, and there are pine needles in my hair.

"I have homework," I say, and as soon as I say it, I see Mom's face clamp down, like a briefcase closing.

"Fine," she says, and she looks again at the TV. Anne glares at me.

"Forget my homework," I say. "I'll shower and come back."

"The movie will be over," Mom says. "And then your father will be here." This time she doesn't even turn her head.

Upstairs I take a brush to my hair and watch four pine

52

needles fall to the ground. I gather them, fold them inside a tissue so Mom doesn't see them, and throw them in the wastebasket. On second thought I pull them back out, pick up my Polaroid, and snap a picture. They are evidence that someone wants me, something I may need a reminder of in the future.

At Dad's that weekend I dress for the party in his tiny bathroom. Some sophomore guy's parents are out of town. I wear tight jeans, and a top showing my belly button. I carefully apply eyeliner and lip gloss. When I am ready, I emerge from the bathroom to find Dad on the futon in front of the TV. Dana is in the kitchen, and Anne is in the chair in the living room, reading. She eyes me. Dad looks me up and down, a surprised expression on his face.

"Whoa," he says.

I put up my hand. "No comments, please," I tell him. I try to move fast, gathering stuff for my purse—money, lip gloss, keys, cell phone—so Dad doesn't look too long. It feels funny having him see me made up like this.

"Remember those cute overalls you used to wear?" Dad turns off the TV. Oh, boy. Here we go.

"Dad, that was ages ago."

"No," he says. "That was last year."

"Whatever," I say.

He pats the cushion next to him, and I sit down. I look

53

at Anne, but she seems to be engrossed in her book.

"Dad, what?" I say. "I have to meet Elisabeth at a party."

"Elisabeth can wait," he says, looking at me earnestly. Out of the corner of my eye I see Dana move toward the living room, see us talking, and back up again into the kitchen. "I don't want you going out like this."

I stand up. "Like what?"

"Jessica," Dad says, his voice getting louder. "Sit down."

I do, but I sit at the edge of the futon, ready to spring. Anne marks her place in the book and gets up, giving us an annoyed look. She goes into the bathroom.

"I said I don't want you looking like this."

"And I said, Like what?"

"Like some kind of tramp, Jessica," he says. I stare at him. I can't believe he said that to me. Part of me wants to tell him how hurtful it is. I mean, he's supposed to be on my side. I've been on his for so long. But the other part, knowing he won't understand and how hypocritical he is, rears its head. I stand up.

"Why not?" I say, and as I do, I look directly at Dana, who is watching from the other room. "Because I look too much like the girls you date?" I can't read Dana's face, but when I look back at Dad, I see a vein protruding from his temple. I feel bad about Dana, especially after our conversation last time, but I knew those words would get him.

"You get changed right now," he says in a low voice.

I grab my purse and my backpack, and I head for the door. "Screw you," I say as I leave.

Once outside I can't control the tears. They rush out in ugly spurts. I sit on the cement stairs and dig into my purse for my compact and a tissue. I listen for Dad to come after me, to not let me go, but he doesn't. He stays inside with Dana. Probably relieved to have me gone. I do my best to fix my makeup.

A few cars pass on the street. I briefly consider calling Ted, forgetting the party, and having him pick me up, a sure way to feel like someone wants me. But I resist the urge, and I call Elisabeth for a ride.

An hour into the party Jason approaches me. He's drunk again. I pretend I am too. We make our way into a bedroom. It's a girl's bedroom. Yellow walls and a frilly canopy. A teddy bear wearing a hot-pink half shirt is propped against a pillow. Jason pushes me down on the bed, and we kiss. I encourage him to touch me, everywhere, anywhere. Just as long as he touches me. This time I am determined to make him like me.

I get myself on top of him and grab his hair as I kiss him. Then I creep my hand down to his fly and unzip. His eyes are closed, his mouth slack. I kiss my way down to his belly, listening as his breathing intensifies and quickens. Listening as he becomes helpless. All mine. His penis is hard and warm, just like Ted's. It is just as velvety soft. I breathe on it, watching it throb a bit. And, before I can take it in my mouth and show off my new skill, Jason squirms and moans and finishes on his boxers.

He swears. Then he jumps up and yanks at his jeans.

"Where are you going?" I ask.

"Back to the party," he says. "Where do you think?"

"But we just got here," I say. I move toward him, and he steps back. He reaches for the doorknob.

"See you around," he says, and he's gone.

Then it's just me and the teddy bear, sitting on the frilly bed. I pick up the bear and hold it to me. I wonder what would happen if the girl who sleeps here came in to find me hugging her teddy bear, curled up on her bed. Maybe she would scream, and the whole party would come upstairs to see what happened. Jason would push his way through the crowd, climb onto the bed, and take me in his arms. I'm sorry, he would say. I shouldn't have left you here alone. It's just . . . it's just I love you, and the feelings scared me. But I'm here now, and I'm ready to be with you. The crowd applauds. Credits roll.

I'll have to remember that one when I can't fall asleep.

Downstairs I can't find Elisabeth. I check the bathroom, the kitchen, every room of the party. Finally I ask a sophomore guy.

"The flat-chested one with short dark hair?" he asks.

I nod. "She's not completely flat," I add defensively.

"She's been gone for a while," he says. "I'm guessing she left."

I go to find my purse. My backpack is in Elisabeth's mother's car. I was going to stay the night. Now I'll have to sneak into Dad's apartment and pray no one wakes up. My throat gets tight like I'm going to cry. Could this night get any worse?

In the kitchen I call for a cab. Jason and a few others are playing quarters at the kitchen table. As I walk away, he looks up.

"You leaving?" he asks.

I nod. *As if you care,* I think. But I also consider the possibility that he does. Maybe my fantasy wasn't entirely off the mark.

"Okay," he says. "See ya Monday."

And with that the night is recovered, perhaps not a complete disaster after all.

I slip the key in the lock, turn the knob slowly, and tiptoe inside. Moonlight splashes through the room, and I see Anne asleep beneath the covers on the futon, her body rising with each breath. I close the door and set my purse on a chair. I pull off my boots. As I turn toward the bathroom, Anne turns over.

"I thought you were sleeping out," she whispers.

"So did I," I whisper back. "Elisabeth left me stranded."

"Why?"

"I don't know," I lie. I know exactly why, but I'm not going to tell Anne any of it.

She sits up. Her hair is mussed. Her glasses are on the floor beside her. She looks pretty right now, with the moonlight on her face.

"How has it been?" I ask, a grimace on my face.

Anne frowns. "Jessie," she says. Nobody's called me Jessie in years. "It's not good."

I come closer. "What?"

She takes the sheet and squeezes it in her fist. "They're getting married," she says.

I make a face. "No way," I say. "He wouldn't tell you without me there."

"I overheard them," Anne says. "Dana wanted to know when he was going to tell us."

I shake my head. "The perfect end to a perfect night," I say.

"I don't know what to do," Anne says, looking at the sheet in her hand.

"What are you talking about?" I say. "There's nothing for you to do."

"About Mom," she says. She looks like she might start crying.

"God, Anne," I say. I pull off my bracelets and throw them on the floor. "Mom's a big girl."

Tears come into Anne's eyes. I stare at her, dumb-founded.

"When are you going to get a life of your own?" I ask. My voice sounds mean, and I know I'm stepping on dangerous ground. We don't talk about this ever. Something about the darkness of the room and the moonlight make me feel brave. Or maybe it's the events of the night.

Anne looks down at the sheet again. "I have my own life," she says. Even she doesn't sound convinced.

"You're sixteen," I say. "You should be hanging out with friends and having fun. Not spending all your time with your mother."

Anne doesn't say anything. The words tumble inside me, out of control. I could go on and on. It's a relief to be saying them, even as it's scary.

"She's using you," I say then.

"She is not."

Anne is fully crying now. I should stop, let her be. But I want her to get it already. I want someone in this family other than me to deal with reality. I'm tired of bearing the weight myself.

"She only cares about herself," I say.

"That's not true."

"Does she ever talk to you about you?" I ask.

Anne is silent, the tears flowing. *Stop,* I command myself. But I can't seem to.

"You have one friend in the world," I tell her. "And she couldn't care less about you."

Anne turns from me, sobbing audibly. *Happy now?* I ask myself. Someone rouses in the other room, and the bedroom door opens.

"Everything okay out here?" Dad asks. He's wearing a bathrobe, and he looks disoriented, woken from a deep sleep. Just seeing him there, bleary-eyed and ignorant, makes me mad.

"We're fine," I say angrily. Anne pulls the blanket up, trying to quiet her sobs. Any fool can see we're not.

Dad clears his throat. He doesn't even glance at Anne. "Okay then," he says. He disappears into the bedroom.

That's about all I can take for one night. I stomp into the bathroom, no longer caring who I disturb.

CHAPTER 7

I finally get Elisabeth on the phone.

"Lizzie," I say. "Talk to me."

"I'm too mad to talk," she says. I can hear a vacuum in the background. She always cleans when she's mad.

"You're the one who left me," I say. "I had to pay for a cab and sneak into my dad's apartment."

"You deserved it," she says.

"Because I like Jason?"

"Because you keep encouraging him to treat you like dirt."

I hear Mom and Anne talking in Mom's room. Mom's voice is rising, which means Anne must have told her about Dad and Dana. He officially told us their wedding plans right before dropping us off. I close my door so I don't have to hear anymore.

"That's not what I'm doing."

Elisabeth sighs. "I can't accommodate it anymore, Jess," she says.

I hate when she gets all codependent-no-more. "I'm not some drug addict," I say.

"Well, you're acting like one," she says. "Your drug of choice is Jason."

I take a deep breath. I want to tell her how he said, "See ya Monday," but I know she'll misinterpret it. Besides, it's easy for her. She has Deb, who supports her no matter what, who cares about what's happening in her life. So I change the subject.

"My dad's getting married, Lizzie," I tell her.

"Oh, no," she says. I hear the vacuum shut down.

"And Mom's losing it."

"I'm too mad for you to be in the middle of a crisis," she tells me. Then, "What can I do?"

"Just tolerate me a little longer," I say.

She sighs. "You know I will."

On Monday Ruth floats through art class, checking out everyone's still-life sketches. We're supposed to draw the pile of squash sitting on a stool in the center of the room. Ashley and her friends keep giggling because one of the vegetables looks phallic. I keep glancing at her, trying to decide how I will ask her what Jason has said about me.

She must know something, but she hasn't looked at me once.

"Just another month and a half," Ruth says as she passes me.

Great. A swift, painful reminder of my complete lack of talent.

I watch as Ashley asks to go to the restroom. Suddenly I have to go too.

In the bathroom I see Ashley's shoes underneath the stall door.

"Great party Saturday night," I say.

"Please," Ashley says. "Fast-forward to me hanging over the toilet bowl Sunday morning."

"Jason must have had a rough morning too," I say, seeing my opening. "He was pretty drunk."

She flushes. I quickly dig into my purse, then apply lip gloss.

"I guess," Ashley says. She emerges from the stall and watches herself in the mirror as she washes her hands. Her hair is blond and blown perfectly straight. She is the Barbie doll of our school. I turn from the mirror, hating to see myself in comparison to her.

"Did he say anything?" I ask.

"About what?"

"About me?"

Ashley examines me. "Sweetie," she says. "What's up?"

I shrug.

"Listen, Jessica," she says. "Do yourself a favor and do not fall for Jason Reilly."

I shake my head. "Of course not," I say. She heads for the door, and I follow. Easy for her to say. Shane, the second-cutest guy in the ninth grade, is in love with her.

"Stick to photography," she says as we get to the art classroom. "Isn't there some kind of contest coming up?"

Jason is in line in the cafeteria when I get there. I keep my eye on him as I move through the line. When he heads for his table, tray in hand, I make my move.

"Can I talk to you?" I ask. "Privately?"

He looks at his tray, then at the table of his friends waiting.

"Uh, yeah," he says. "I guess for a minute."

I lead him to an unoccupied table, the one where Tiffany usually eats alone. He eyes it uncomfortably, then hesitantly sets down the tray. I wait for him to sit, but realize he doesn't plan to.

"Where are we going?" I ask.

He shrugs. "I don't know about you, but I was planning to sit with my friends and have some lunch."

Very funny.

"You know what I mean," I say. I watch him, remembering the taste of his mouth, remembering how he was under my spell on that little girl's bed.

"What do you want from me?" he says.

"It's just that you and I were together Saturday," I say. "And a few weeks before too."

A couple of people give us curious glances. They're not used to seeing us together.

"So what?" he says. He shifts his feet, growing restless. "We had some fun."

I bite my lip.

"What?" he says. "You thought we were something more?"

I look down.

"I've got to get back to my table," he says. He grabs his tray and moves quickly, before I have a chance to say anything more.

Rather than stay after school to work in the darkroom, I go straight home. I don't want to see Ruth again. I don't want her to ask me about the contest or, worse, Jason. At home it seems like no one is there until I get upstairs. Mom and Anne are in Mom's bedroom, and Mom is crying. Again. I can feel something rise in my throat: frustration, disgust, sick-of-it-all-ness. Only when it reaches my mouth do I realize it's a scream.

Anne comes rushing out of the room.

"What's going on?" she says.

"God," I yell. "How can you stand it?"

"What's the matter with you?"

"What's the matter with me?" I ask. "What's the matter with *you*?"

Mom comes up behind Anne. Her eyes are puffy and red.

"Calm down, Jessica," she says in a steady voice.

"And you," I yell. "I can't even look at you."

I stomp into my room, slamming the door behind me. In my mind I see Jason walking away. *You thought we were something more?* An ache spreads in my chest and flows all the way to my fingertips. No wonder I can't stand Mom's crying anymore. I'm just as needy as she is.

I dial the number and wait for him to pick up.

"Come get me," I say. "I want to go to your place."

In ten minutes, just enough time for me to change into the black miniskirt and reapply my makeup, the silver Civic pulls up in front of the Gibbonses' house.

Ted's apartment is just one room with a tiny kitchen and bathroom. There's no closet, and his clothes clump together in two piles against the wall. A tapestry hangs from tacks above them. His unmade bed is the main attraction of the room. He moves past me and pulls two beers from the fridge. Then he motions toward the bed.

"Make yourself comfortable," he says. He takes a long swig from the beer and hands one to me.

I sit, my heart thrumming. I look down at the brown shag carpet and try to steady my breathing. *What am I doing here?* I go over the events of the day: Ashley's airy disinterest, Jason's flat-out rejection, and my mother's crying to Anne. The events don't actually come to me one by one. They come as a wave of feeling. A wave of dejection and anxiety about not mattering to anyone. Except, perhaps, Ted.

"I thought I'd never get you here," he says. He sits next to me and pushes my hair behind my ear. He kisses the ear gently, so gently the kiss touches me deep down, where I feel invisible, where a tiny version of me waits to be seen. I feel like I might cry.

"Well," I say. "I'm here now."

He takes my beer and places it on the floor. We kiss. With my eyes closed, his touch feels like oxygen, like puffs of breath bringing me back into being. He pushes up my shirt and unsnaps my bra. Slides his hands under my skirt. He pulls his shirt over his head and yanks down his jeans. It all happens quickly. And suddenly we're naked, except for my skirt hiked up around my stomach, and he is pressing, struggling to get inside me. *Inside* me. I hold my breath and grit my teeth. This is, of course, my first time.

Ted pulls back to look at me. "You've done this before, right?" he asks.

I try to look at ease. An eighteen-year-old would have done this before.

"Of course," I say.

He regards me a moment longer. I look to the side, where I have a full view of the kitchen, just in case my face reveals more than I want it to. A crusted-over plate and fork sit next to the sink.

"How old are you?" Ted asks. "Really."

"I told you," I say, still looking at the kitchen. "I'm eighteen."

"Because right now would be the time to tell me if you weren't."

I still can't look at him. I consider this. Telling him will lead to him removing his hands. It will wind up with him going away for good. I can't risk it, not with the wave rushing through my body. Not when his touch can inflate me, make me feel seen.

"It's just been a while," I say.

He's still looking at me, trying to ascertain the truth.

"I want you to," I say then.

And with that, Ted acquiesces. He pushes harder. It hurts. A lot. Enough that I feel tears come into my eyes. I squeeze them shut, and a tear rolls down my face. It lands in my ear. I know I'm dead set on being eighteen, but I feel like a little girl. I grip the sheet, pulling it into a ball inside my fist. After a bit the pain settles into numbness.

Eons later Ted shudders and moans, and rolls off me. Well, that's that. I pull the sheet up over myself. I feel warm liquid down there, and I remember, with a start, that girls can bleed their first time.

"Can I use your bathroom?" I whisper.

"Of course," he mumbles. When I look at him, I see his eyes are closed. He breathes peacefully, falling asleep.

I hold the sheet to me while I gather up my clothes. I push down my skirt and snap on my bra. I go into his bathroom. A couple of magazines—the same kind I saw in his car—sit on the back of the toilet. I rip off some toilet paper and lower the seat. When I pee, it stings, and I bite my hand to keep from making a noise. There is no blood. I throw on the rest of my clothes, and, careful to avoid the mirror as I leave the bathroom, I tiptoe past sleeping Ted, grab my purse, and get out of there.

Outside, the air is cold. It is almost dark, that blue time of day that I love. Goose bumps form on my legs. Why did I wear this stupid miniskirt again? The leaves sway in a silent dance as they fall from the trees. A candy wrapper skitters across the street. A car passes. The world is exactly the same. Impossible, but true. Everyone says your first time should be magical. You should be in love. You should feel safe. Because you can't go back once you've done it. That will always be your first time. Years later this is what I'll remember as my first time. That inflated sensation is long gone. Now I just feel vaguely nauseous; it's the feeling I get when reality dawns.

I call a taxicab.

At home Mom's minivan is gone and the house is silent. I stand a moment in the foyer, listening to the buzz from the refrigerator. I climb the stairs. My legs feel like lead. I strip my clothes off and turn on the shower, nice and hot. I've read about girls bathing with superhot water after rape, trying to scrub off their perpetrator. But I went willingly into it. I pushed for it. The water feels good. Comforting. It washes away these thoughts and the anxiety accompanying them. In fact, I feel exhausted. What I want more than anything is to get into my bed and close my eyes.

But before I do, I take the miniskirt and dump it in the garbage.

CHAPTER 8

Something's wrong," I hear someone say the next morning. The voice starts in my dream. I'm at the edge of a lake with Tiffany, watching a bunch of men ride their motorcycles, one after another, into the water. Some jump off just in time, but most go into the water with their bikes, and they don't come back up. Tiffany and I are cheering, but I can feel anxiety racing like a mouse in my chest. *Something's wrong*, someone says, and I turn to agree, relieved someone else notices.

I open my eyes to see Anne there. Mom is coming in behind her, holding a thermometer. My room looks fuzzy, and my blankets feel heavy and hot.

"Look at her," Anne says.

"What?" I start to say, but the pain in my throat makes me close my mouth quickly.

"Open up," Mom says. She slips the thermometer into my mouth. "Anne, go get a cool towel." Anne disappears and returns with the towel. The thermometer beeps, and Mom pulls it. "Yup," she says. "A hundred and two."

Anne places the towel on my forehead, and I let my eyes fall closed. It feels nice. How can she care for me after all I said to her last week at Dad's? I'm a rotten sister. I'm a rotten lot of things, actually.

"I'll call the school," Mom says. I lift a heavy arm and touch her.

"Don't go yet," I whisper. I wince and reach for my throat.

"Honey," Mom says. Her brow is knitted, concerned. "Let me at least get you a lozenge." I hold on to her arm. "I promise to be right back," she says with a smile.

In the afternoon I wake again to see Mom on the floor by my bed, looking at a *Vogue* she found on my nightstand. I can see a woman's full red lips and strong cheekbones on the glossy page she's examining. She turns when she hears me.

"How are you feeling?" she asks.

"Like crap," I tell her. At least I can talk without knives ripping at my throat.

She hands me a lozenge. When I lift my head, it pounds.

She watches me.

"Can I help you?" I whisper.

"We haven't spent time together in a while," she says.

Whatever guilt I had about being rotten has obviously taken a backseat. Even with the flu I can feel my shield form.

"We're not spending time together," I say. "You're taking care of me."

"Well," she says.

I don't say anything. I vaguely remember wanting her to stay with me earlier. A fever does that: clouds judgment.

"I'm doing much better since learning of your father's engagement," she says, like I asked. "I can even talk about it now if you want."

"Yeah," I say. "That's what I want."

"I think it will be good for us." Apparently she doesn't get sarcasm. I close my eyes and wipe a sweaty strand of hair off my forehead. "It will help us move on."

"Define 'us,'" I say.

"All of us," she says. "You, Anne, me. Even your father."

"Mom," I say, "everyone's moved on but you. Don't you see that?"

She looks at me. I can practically hear her brain rumbling, trying to fit what I've said into her own version of reality, where she is the star and everyone else is just an extension of her.

"It sounds like your fever broke," she says. I sigh. She's not going to get it. She hands me the thermometer, and I put it in my mouth. In the silence, yesterday begins to creep into my consciousness. Ted's apartment. His hands. The stinging pee. I push the covers down. They're making me sweat. The thermometer beeps.

"Ninety-seven," Mom says. "I guess you're going to live."

"Hooray," I say.

Mom smiles, missing the sarcasm once again.

Later I crawl out of bed and set my camera timer. Christiane Nill has a famous self-portrait of her distorted face in a glass. Maybe that's the approach I need: myself distorted, sick with the flu. I lie back on the bed, exhausted from all the energy it took to set up the shot. I wait for the *snap!* Then I rouse myself to set the timer again. After nine snapshots I have to break for a nap.

When I wake in the evening, I feel a little better and very hungry. I can hear the TV in the family room and music coming from Anne's room. I head to the kitchen to find some food.

"There's some leftover chicken and rice in the fridge," Mom calls from the family room. I take the leftovers out and open a cabinet for a plate. Out the window I see the silver Civic parked beneath a streetlamp. He is watching the Gibbonses' house. My heart jumps into my throat. I step away from the window. Part of me wants to go out there. Let him see me in sweats and no makeup. Let him see that I'm only fourteen, too young to have done what we did. Too young to regret that I did.

"Did you find it?" Mom asks. She's still watching her show, unaware.

I tell her I did and pop my plate into the microwave. I wonder if she would even care if she knew.

Right then the Gibbonses' Volvo wagon pulls onto the street and then into their driveway. Mrs. Gibbons jumps out of the car and opens the back door to get the twins. Mr. Gibbons comes out the front door to help with grocery bags. I watch, horrified, as he registers Ted watching them. I put a hand over my mouth so as not to make any sound.

Mr. Gibbons walks to the Civic. They exchange some words. Ted scans the street. Then he starts the engine and takes off. Mr. Gibbons looks directly at our house. In the light of the streetlamp I can't see his expression. But I know enough to stand clear of the window. I take a few deep breaths, my mind racing.

Sure enough, the doorbell rings. I stay perfectly still as I hear Mom go to the door, unlock it, and greet Mr. Gibbons. He apologizes for coming to the door so late in the evening.

Then he says, "I want to make you aware of a little situation. Some man was asking after your daughter Jessica."

Oh, God.

"Oh?" Mom asks. Her voice is tight. I can just imagine what she's thinking. She doesn't like to look like she doesn't know things.

"He thought she lived at our house."

"Is that so?"

"I want you to know I didn't tell him where she lives."

"I appreciate that," Mom says.

They exchange good-byes, and the door closes. I eat my food at the table, pretending to be calm. I consider telling Mom. This is, after all, the opportune time. But as soon as she appears in the doorway, wearing her dismayed-parent look, I know I'll tell her nothing.

"Mr. Gibbons says there's some man asking about you at their house."

I look up, feigning surprise and confusion. "Me?"

"What do you know about this, Jessica?"

I shake my head, chewing. "Nothing," I say. "I swear."

"I don't appreciate being lied to," she says.

"I don't know anything," I tell her again.

"That was embarrassing for me," Mom says. "Having some stranger tell me about my own daughter."

"He's not a stranger," I say. "It's Mr. Gibbons."

"Are you suggesting you know what this is about?"

"I'm suggesting you're being dramatic."

Mom watches me, trying to decide whether to believe me. I take another bite of chicken, avoiding her gaze.

"I don't know what I would do if I found out you were sneaking around with someone."

I look up at her.

"Just like your father."

Exactly. I look back down.

"Relax," I tell her. "There's nothing for you to know."

And with that, she finally leaves the room.

Friday, feeling better, I go to the darkroom with a full roll of self-portraits. I was so woozy and out of it when I took the shots, I have no idea what they will look like. The possibility is exciting. Finally I may have what I've been chasing. If they're not perfect, I can always change them a bit after the fact. Even Ansel Adams knew sometimes you have to use techniques to get to what you see. The camera's first shot doesn't always reveal everything you want to show.

I make the prints, dip, and hang them with clothespins. The first pictures confuse me as they begin to take shape. Is that me on my bed? A wave of heat washes through me as I remember. The photos I took of Ted in the park woods. I pull them down—two of them—and tuck them in my bag. I don't want to look at him right now.

The photos of me reveal themselves. In each, my eyes are hollowed out and shaded with dark circles. My skin is pale. My hair sticks up. The bed is a wrinkled mess beneath my head. When I'm not looking at the camera, I appear dead, a corpse. That is closer to my goal. It's not exactly right, but a month before the contest, with nothing else started, I decide I will work with it.

So when I run into Ruth before I leave, the photos in hand, I am not full of anxiety and dread. This is new.

Ruth smiles big. She's wearing a corduroy jumper, a turtleneck, and her signature Birkenstocks. A student is with her, a freshman from art class, carrying a canvas.

"I thought you had fallen off the planet," Ruth says to me.

"I was sick." It feels nice to not have to lie.

"You look in good spirits today," she says.

"My photograph is coming along," I tell her.

The student watches me. Her brow is furrowed, and she holds the canvas so I can't see what's on it. Ruth introduces her, and explains she's working on a painting for the contest. That's why she looks angry. That's why she's hiding her work. She knows Ruth's got me pegged to win. I wish.

When they leave, I wish the girl luck. She smiles, but she doesn't wish me the same.

"I was awesome," Elisabeth says. She's pacing in my room, something she does when she's excited. I'm on my bed. We're back here after her track meet, where she came in second, running just under a six-minute mile. I was watching from the bleachers, surrounded by parents and classmates.

She's been talking about this meet since school started. I knew I had to be there if I wanted to salvage our friendship. Which, of course, I do.

"You were awesome," I say. "You always are."

She smiles and pushes her newly washed hair from her eyes. She stops at my desk, where my bag sits. She tugs at something I can't see that's sticking out from the opening.

"Jess," she says. "Who's this?"

I jump from the bed. I forgot about those pictures. I take them from her.

"Nobody," I say. "Some guy in the park. It's for an assignment."

Elisabeth studies me. She puts her hand out. "Let me see it."

"They're really bad," I say, holding them behind my back.

"I don't care," she says. Her hand stays extended. I swallow and hand her the photos. She flips through them, one, then the other. Ted is flushed, eager, animal-like. He looks at the camera with fierce desire. I captured the moment perfectly. Elisabeth looks at me again, and I keep my eyes on the photos, hoping she can't catch anything in my expression.

"Jess," Elisabeth says again. "Tell me who this is."

"I told you," I say. "Some guy."

"You're getting awfully good at this," she says. She hands back the pictures.

"At photography?" I ask, hopeful.

"At lying," she says. Then she gathers up her things.

"Lizzie," I say.

"I've been such a good friend to you," she says.

"I know that."

"I stood by you when your dad moved out and you found out there was another woman."

"Yes," I say, but she won't let me talk.

"I was the only one who understood when you lost your camera that time."

"You were," I say.

"And all I get back are your lies."

"I don't want—"

She cuts me off again. "I've had it, Jessica. I don't deserve this. If you want to alienate me, I can't stop you."

"That's not what I want," I say.

"That's sure how it feels," she says. She walks out of my room. A half minute later I hear her leave through the front door.

CHAPTER 9

The saleswoman flits around Anne and me. Dana stands in front of us, her hands clasped before her. It seems she's forgotten about the comment I made to Dad.

"You look beautiful," she says.

Anne keeps her arms folded over her chest. Her anger clashes badly with the periwinkle satin bridesmaid dress.

"We look like ugly oversize dolls," she whispers to me.

I frown. "Speak for yourself," I say. But then I turn to the mirror. Anne's right. There's nothing subtle about these dresses. Surprising choice for an artist. I twist my hair and hold it up, seeing if the image looks any more normal. Two days of unshaved underarm hair glares back at me. I quickly drop my arms.

"How's it going back there?" Dad calls from his post

near the front of the store. He's been standing there since we arrived, awkwardly holding his newspaper. It's hard to believe this is the same man who robotically moved grocery bags from Mom's car to the kitchen, then quickly disappeared.

"Come see," Dana says. "They look like princesses."

Anne snorts. Dad appears around the side of the mirror.

"Oh, my," Dad says. He stares at us, looking a little misty. "Are these really my girls?"

"Dad, please," I say. "The 'Sunrise, Sunset' routine is getting old."

"He loves you girls so much," Dana says. They share a look. Is she kidding me?

"Can we just get out of these?" I say.

Anne doesn't wait for a response. She goes back into the dressing room, and I can see under the curtain that she stomps on the dress as it drops.

Later, when we're back in Dad's apartment, Dana motions for me to follow her into Dad's bedroom. I'm hesitant. I don't want to see their soon-to-be-conjugal bed. But I'm curious what she's up to. Leaning against the wall are two canvasses. They are both abstract landscapes, the colors rich and suggestive.

"These are yours?" I ask. I try not to sound too surprised. They are beautiful.

"What do you think?" She bites the side of her cheek

and looks from me to the paintings. She seriously wants my opinion.

"I think they're magnificent," I say.

We are both silent a moment, examining the paintings.

"The color alone makes it look like those hills are in the background," I tell her.

"Exactly," she says. "So it works."

"Definitely."

"It's a series I'm working on." she says. "On color and perspective."

I nod my head. "I really like it."

She smiles at me. "Thanks," she says. "I'd still like to see what you're working on."

"I'm trying to get something together for a contest," I say.

Dana sits on the edge of the bed. Thank God it's made.

"A contest," Dana says, urging me to say more. I'm surprised to find myself talking to her like this, but it feels right. She's genuinely interested.

"I have to come up with a self-portrait."

"Wow," she says, nodding. "That's a challenge."

"Especially when I don't really know who I am." This last part just flies out. Dana is silent, watching me. I look at the carpeted floor, wishing I hadn't said it.

"Don't feel bad," she says. "I still don't know who I am, and I'm in my thirties."

I press my sneaker over a stain on the floor.

"I'd be happy to help you explore your self-portrait," she says.

I nod. "That would be nice," I say, and I mean it.

Mr. Weiss stands at the blackboard, madly marking numbers and xs like he's unlocking a secret code. He's young with thick, black curls, and glasses. Rumor has it he sleeps with his students. Of course, the latest one is assumed to be Tiffany. She sits in the front row wearing tight jeans and a low-cut top. Her breasts are huge, big enough to make woman-size cleavage. Mr. Weiss faces the class, asks for volunteers. Only one person raises his hand, so he picks out three others: Elisabeth, Josh, and me. He never calls on Tiffany. Who knows? Maybe the rumors are true.

The three of us go to the blackboard and start working through problems. Elisabeth has not spoken to me since she left my house last week. This time I can't seem to change her mind. I glance at her, but she ignores me. However, Josh, on my other side, is looking right at me. I try to finish my problem, but his eyes bore into my cheek.

"What," I whisper at him.

"How's it going?" he whispers back, a strange smile on his face.

I shrug. He's Jason's friend. And he's never given me the time of day before.

"You going to Ashley's party this weekend?" He's still wearing that odd smile, like he knows something I don't.

"Josh and Jessica," Mr. Weiss says. "Is there something going on?"

That's what I'd like to know.

"No, sir," Josh says loudly. I hear some giggles behind me. Josh is always going for the laugh. It's hard to find anyone who doesn't like him. He looks at me again, and I glare at him, but I can't get the smile off my lips.

"Well?" he whispers.

I nod, still smiling.

"All right," he says. "I'll see you there."

I finish solving for x, my face hot. Then I sit down, avoiding everyone's eyes.

At home I examine the corpse picture. It is not quite right, still missing something essential, something about who I am. But I can't place what it is. I try turning the picture to the side and squinting at it. Still nothing. I take down my photography book and flip through it, looking for inspiration. Maybe something with color, a blue overlay. I stare at the picture, tapping my lips. I am tempted to call Dana, to take her up on her offer. Just as I am getting up the nerve to do it, there's a knock.

"Phone for you," Anne says.

"Who is it?"

Anne grunts and goes back to the phone. A few seconds later she comes back.

"Some guy named Ted," she says. My heart jumps. I never gave him my phone number. "He wants you to call him."

That kills my concentration. I get up from my desk and stand near the window, almost expecting to see the silver Civic there. At some point I'll have to deal with this. At some point I'll have to tell him I don't want to see him anymore. But a part of me doesn't want that yet. It's how I've felt about Ted from the start: I don't want him too close, but I also don't want him too far. Nobody else pays me the attention he does, and I don't like how it feels to imagine it gone.

So I call him back.

"You lied to me," he says. Nevermind "forget." "Lying" is my new middle name. I wrap my arms around myself defensively. "Why didn't you just tell me where you really live?"

"I don't know," I tell him.

"I don't like being lied to, Jessica." He sounds like my mother. You don't even know what my real lie is, I want to tell him. *I could have you arrested*, I think, *with one phone call.*

"Then why did you call?" I ask.

I hear banging, like he's hammering. It's rhythmic, filling

the silence, and it seems to go on for many minutes.

Finally he says, "I don't know."

The door unlatches, and Mom comes in. I see her through the banister railing. She's carrying a bag of groceries. She has no makeup on, and she looks tired. I wish she cared enough to put on some lipstick or at least some blush. I wish she didn't look so old since Dad moved out. Mom glances up at me, as though she can hear who's on the phone. She eyes me suspiciously.

"I've got to go," I say.

"Of course you do," Ted says. He hangs up before I can say anything else.

Later I call Dana. I pull the phone into my room so Anne can't hear.

Dad is reasonably surprised when I ask for her, but he has the sense to not push for details. Dana and I make a plan to meet at a coffee shop within walking distance.

Dana studies the photo I take from my folder. Immediately I see the flaws. Especially compared to her landscapes.

"It's a stupid idea," I say.

"No," Dana says. Her blond hair is in a bun, and she wears no makeup. I have to admit she's pretty. "It's smart. You look really out of it."

"I was going for dead," I tell her.

She examines it some more. "You'll have to wash out the color a bit more to look truly dead."

I slide the picture to me. She's right. I don't even look close to dead. I sigh. At least she was honest, didn't dance around my feelings.

"A dead self-portrait," Dana says. "I like that."

"Do you?"

She nods. "I'm curious what you mean by it," she says.

I shrug. "I guess I feel dead inside sometimes."

She studies me, just like she did the photograph. I look at my nails and tug on a hangnail. I keep finding myself in these conversations with Dana.

"That's funny," she says. "I don't see that in you."

"You don't?"

"You have too much energy racing through you to be dead."

I look at her. In this short time knowing me she sees this?

"Well," I say, "sometimes the energy goes away."

Dana nods, but I can tell she's unconvinced. Unfortunately so am I. Dana's right. This picture has nothing to do with me. Or if it does, it only scratches the surface. Damn.

Tiffany and I are the only ones on the late bus again. This time she sits just a few rows away. Her shiny dark hair is pulled into a ponytail. It is hard not to think about when we were younger, when we used to braid each other's hair. She turns around.

"I guess everyone else runs home after school," she says. Her voice is deep and raspy.

I shrug. I don't really want to talk to her, regardless of what I was thinking last time we were here.

"What were you doing?" she asks.

"I develop pictures in the darkroom," I say. I am careful not to meet her eyes for too long.

"That's right," she says. "Photography is your thing. I remember that."

I look away at the reference to our past relationship.

"I tutor kids after school."

I nod. Then I smile slightly. "That's nice of you," I say. *Especially,* I think, *when most kids have been nothing but cruel to you for so long.*

She shrugs. "It comes easy to me," she says. She takes a pack of cigarettes out of her bag and taps one out. She offers it to me, but I shake my head. She takes out another and puts it behind her ear.

"You smoke?" I say.

"Only when I'm awake," she says. She laughs at her joke.

"It's a stupid habit," I say.

She shrugs again. "So's being a bitch, but that doesn't stop most girls from being one."

I frown. I'm not sure if she's referring to me or other girls.

"Why are you nice to those people?" she asks me.

"What people?" I ask, though I know exactly who she's talking about now.

"Ashley and her friends."

I look away. "They're my friends."

Tiffany laughs, throwing her head back. The cigarette falls from behind her ear and rolls onto the floor. She grabs it before it gets out of reach, and puts it back. "You think they're your friends?"

"They are," I say.

"Whatever," Tiffany says. "I may not be the most-liked girl in school, but at least I'm not an idiot."

"Screw you," I say. I look out the window, angry I let the school slut talk to me in the first place.

"Suit yourself," she says, and she turns around to gather her things before getting off at her stop.

CHAPTER 10

Elisabeth is at her locker after school. I take a breath and walk toward her.

"Lizzie," I say. She doesn't look at me. She pulls a book from the locker and puts it in her backpack, the same navy blue JanSport she's had since last year.

"Liz, please," I say. "You're my best friend."

She still doesn't speak, but I can see pain in her expression.

"I'm sorry," I say. "I'm really, really sorry."

She slams closed her locker and doesn't look up.

"Liz," I say, getting frustrated. "Is it so bad if I can't help liking boys?"

"Don't you care what people think about you?" she says in a low voice.

I shrug, unsure where she's going with this.

"Everyone's talking," she says. "You're making a fool of yourself."

"Since when do you care what people think?" I say, feeling defensive.

She looks right at me now. "You're acting shameless," she says. Tears pop into her eyes. "I don't know who you are anymore."

She storms off, leaving me alone with my heart in my throat. Join the club, I want to call after her. I head for the exit, just in time to see Jason and his friends huddled in the parking lot. He is never alone, always surrounded by people. He is a wanted guy. I swallow, trying to push down the empty feeling Elisabeth left me with. Maybe we're not friends anymore. Maybe she's left me for good. She wants me to be who I was, but I don't even know how to get back to that girl. She's long gone, kicked aside by the feelings tied up with boys, especially Jason.

Jason, who is right over there.

I see his dirty blond hair glinting in the sun, and my toes tingle with longing.

"Hey, Jessica," someone calls from the huddle. Ashley pokes her head from the group. She waves me over. I smile. Maybe, just maybe, I'm a little wanted too.

"I thought you could settle this," she says when I get there.

"Ash," Shane warns, but Ashley ignores him. Jason looks down at his feet and kicks at a pebble. I try to look relaxed, like I'm not busting inside standing so close to Jason.

Ashley entwines her arm in mine, like we're the best of friends.

"Shane here says when you flush a toilet south of the equator, it swirls in the opposite direction to the way it swirls here," she says.

I shrug. "I guess," I say, confused as to what this has to do with me.

"Is it true?" she asks.

"I don't know," I say.

"Really?" she says. Her friends watch her with anticipation. Something is happening here, something I know nothing about. "I thought you would."

"I've never been south of the equator," I tell her warily.

"That's not what I heard."

At this her friends start to laugh.

"Damnit, Ash," Jason says.

Oh.

"Very funny," I say. My face grows warm. I disentangle my arm from Ashley's.

"Come on," Ashley says. "It was just a joke."

Jason doesn't look at me. My heart sits in my throat. He told everyone, I guess. I thought it was meaningful, something between him and me. Even if we weren't going to have a relationship, it was still ours. Apparently I was wrong. Apparently what happened between us belongs to the whole school. This is what Elisabeth meant when she said people were talking.

"Don't be mad," Ashley says. She's still smiling.

"Whatever," I say, because I don't know what else to say. Because I want to look like I don't care. That's how Jason feels. Why can't I?

When I walk away, I see Tiffany waiting within earshot for her bus. She stares at me, and I glare back until she looks away. I am nothing like you, I want to yell.

At home I try to focus on the photo, but I can't sit still. I put on sneakers and a sweatshirt and head out for a walk. The wind whips my hair around my head. Cars buzz by. Each one has another person with his own story. I see their shadowy faces, then they're gone. A bus rumbles by, showcasing a woman's red, glossy, pouting lips, advertising lipstick. I watch the men who pass, smile when they whistle. Even though walking now feels different, dangerous since Ted. A Volvo wagon slows onto the shoulder. The familiar feelings start up in my body: racing heart, heat in my face. Someone is stopping for me, for *me*, and I can go with him if I choose. I carefully turn my head to get a look at the driver. It's Mr. Gibbons.

"Can I give you a lift home?" he asks when I approach.

"I'm fine," I say. "Just taking a walk." I cross my arms over my chest. I'm afraid of what he thinks of me, ever since that night with Ted.

"Please," Mr. Gibbons says. "It's freezing out there."

"Really," I say. "I want to walk."

Mr. Gibbons looks at me suspiciously. He obviously thinks I'm up to no good. He is about to cede, and I nod my head.

"It is cold," I say. I get in. The black interior is immaculate. Classical music drifts from the speakers. The twins are in their car seats in the back. I smile at them, and one makes a raspberry in my direction.

Mr. Gibbons pulls back into the traffic.

"How are things, Jessica?" he asks.

I shrug. "Okay."

He glances at me.

"Everything okay at home?"

I frown. What is he getting at? "Everything's fine," I tell him.

"Because if you need to talk to anyone . . . ," he says. He clears his throat. "You know Mrs. Gibbons is a counselor."

I stare straight ahead, focusing on the taillights of the car in front of us. My face is very warm. "I'm fine," I try to say, but my voice cracks. I shake my head instead.

He turns off of the freeway. One of the twins squeals. I close my eyes, wishing I had just refused the ride. As soon as he slows in front of my house, I snap open the door.

95

"Jessica," Mr. Gibbons says. He grabs my arm to keep me from fleeing. I wait, one leg out the door. "I didn't mean to upset you," he says. "We were worried."

I nod.

"When we saw that kid waiting for you."

"I don't know him," I blurt.

"We didn't know what to think."

The wind picks up outside, bringing in a blast of cold air, and rustling the leaves on the ground.

"I don't know him," I say again.

"We have small children," Mr. Gibbons says then, his voice lower. "He was sitting outside our house."

I yank my arm from him and step outside the car.

"I don't know him." Tears come into my eyes. I slam the door and turn to run across the street. A car slams on its brakes, and the woman inside, a woman I recognize from our block, throws her arms into the air. She stares at me, her eyes wide and frightened, like I'm some kind of monster. I run past her toward my house.

Jason is the first person I see as I enter the party. He's got his arm around Ashley's friend, talking with a few others. The girl looks right at me. My throat tightens. This is not a good start to the night. First I had to come alone because Elisabeth is mad at me. Now I have to see Jason cuddling with some girl. I head for the kitchen, determined to have an okay time. The girl who was with Ruth is there. Great. "Jessica, right?" she says.

I nod and move past her, hoping she'll get the hint.

"We're both in Ruth's class," she says. "We met the other day."

I grab a beer and lean against the counter. Obviously there's no fighting this.

"I'm so nervous about the contest," she says. She has straight black hair and dark skin. She's pretty.

"Me too," I tell her.

"You?" she asks. "Why would you be nervous?"

"Why wouldn't I be?"

Josh comes through the kitchen. He grabs a beer, watching me. I smile and look away. This night is looking up.

"You're so good," the girl says. "I've seen what you do."

"I'm not good," I tell her. "And I have nothing worthwhile for the contest."

She frowns, looking concerned. Maybe I was wrong about her. "Don't say that about yourself," she says quietly.

"Better me than somebody else."

The girl watches me. I can tell she doesn't know what to say. What? I want to say. You've never talked to a person with wavering self-worth before? I look past her, hoping she'll pick up on my hint this time.

"Good luck with your photograph," she says softly before she walks away. I try to look casual. I can't help but glance at her once more. I never even asked her name. No wonder my friend count is at zero right now. I down my beer and turn to find Josh.

He's hanging out with a group of friends, including Jason. Jason still has his arm around that girl. I arrange my shirt so that my bra strap is showing. Then I approach. The music is loud. The bass pounds beneath my feet. Josh turns to face me. He has short brown hair and freckles. He's not gorgeous, but he's got nice eyes that twinkle when he smiles. Which he does now. He puts his arm over my shoulder. Jason notices.

"You all know Jessica, right?" Josh says.

I look right at Jason, but he looks away. That old feeling tugs at my throat. How is it I can feel such longing for what was between us, and he doesn't? I wish more than anything I could go back in time, fix the ugly parts of me that made him turn away.

"We're new friends," Josh says. "Isn't that right?" he asks me.

"Sure," I say. Jason says something to the girl he's with, but I can't hear. I put my arm around Josh.

"You don't have anything to drink," Josh says. "We'll have to fix that."

He steers me toward the kitchen, and I see Elisabeth. She sees me, too, with Josh, our arms around each other. She shakes her head. I'm beginning to think I was right. It wasn't just Jason. It's any guy. She's mad because things have changed. I think of her pink room, the dolls on the shelf. She wants everything to stay the way it was. The truth is there are things about the old days I miss too. But you can't stop time. She, of all people, should know this. It doesn't matter how childlike she keeps her room. Her father's death will keep getting farther and farther away.

Josh pulls a beer from the cooler, pops the top, and hands it to me.

"Drink up," he says. His breath is warm on my cheek and it smells of beer. He holds his face there while I take a sip.

"Let's go back to your friends," I say. I'm thinking, of course, about Jason.

"Let's not and say we did," Josh says, still close to my cheek. I turn my head to look at him. He's wearing a grin.

"What did you have in mind?" I ask.

"You, me, and an empty room," he says.

Jason passes us, his arm still tight around that girl.

"Lead the way," I tell Josh.

We make our way past the crowd and up the same stairs, where Jason and I had been hand in hand. The feeling sits like something solid in my throat. It's the same feeling I had with Ted. The same one that swells when I see Jason. I can't get Josh's hands on me fast enough. We start kissing as soon as we're behind the door.

His tongue is clumsy, nothing like Jason's. His breath is

sour. I keep my eyes closed tight and hold my breath. I let his hands snake along my waist and up my shirt.

"I hear you give blow jobs," he whispers.

I pull back. "What?"

"And that you're good," he says, trying to pull me back. He presses a bit on my head. "What do you say?"

I try to pry his hands from me. "I say I have to go."

He grips a little tighter. "Come on," he says. "You did it for Jay."

It starts to dawn on me. Jason told his friends I was an easy blow job. That's all I was this whole time. I feel like I might start crying. "No," I say. He won't release his hands. "Let me go."

"What's your problem?" he says, angry now.

"My problem is that you're still touching me," I say. Finally he releases me.

He swears at me as I race out of the room, but I barely hear him. I'm running down the stairs, past the crowd of people, past the confused looks of Elisabeth and the girl with the painting, past Jason who doesn't even look my way, and out the door into the cold air. Only then do I let myself cry.

Once and for all I see who I am. I don't even need my camera for it. I am rotten to my family, worthless to my friends, and dirty to boys. No wonder no one can love me. There's nothing there to love.

CHAPTER 11

The next day I stay in bed until two o'clock. Mom knocks on my door a few times, but I just groan and roll over. She seems to know to stay away. She leaves me a tray of food, but eating feels like a luxury. Something I don't deserve. I sit by the window and watch the few leaves left on the trees as they spin and thrash in the wind and finally float down to the street below.

Just as the afternoon begins to turn blue, the phone rings, and Anne comes into my room.

"Guess who that was," she says.

I don't answer. I don't want to know.

"Dana. She's coming to pick you up."

I groan. "I'm not going anywhere," I say.

"I told her you hadn't left your room all day. She said

she's coming to get you." Anne looks amused. "I guess she thinks she can help." She snorts.

"She's not that bad, Anne."

"Maybe not to you."

"Oh, right," I say. "What has she done to you?"

"Nothing much," Anne says. "Just stole Dad away from this family."

I stand and grab my jeans from the floor.

"Don't be so dramatic," I say. "Dad didn't leave just to get with Dana."

"Oh no?" she says. Her voice is high pitched and ugly. Her face is red like it gets before she might cry. "Then why did he leave?"

"Unlike you," I say, "he had enough of Mom."

Anne walks away. She doesn't want to go near this conversation with me again. The truth is, I don't either. Dad didn't handle himself any better than Mom. It's just been my job to carry his weight since he left.

"You're lucky Mom's at the store," Anne calls from the hallway.

"She's got to face reality eventually," I yell back. "Now's as good a time as any."

I change into jeans. I put my hair in a ponytail. Now I'm extra glad Dana's coming to get me out of here. Thank you, Anne.

Dana doesn't say much once I'm in her Jetta. She just smiles and drives.

"Where are we going?" I ask.

"You'll see."

After a bit we park in front of an old warehouse. I follow her inside. People mill about with wine glasses. A table is set up with platters of cheeses and olives. On the walls, framed photos hang, each lit up by an individual light that fans down from the ceiling. Dana's taken me to a gallery.

"My friend's opening night," Dana says, her arms spread wide, gesturing to the large industrial space. "She's a photographer."

"Oh," I say. I'm genuinely surprised.

"Dana." A woman Mom's age approaches. "You came."

She and Dana hug. "I wouldn't have missed it," Dana says. "And I brought a friend."

She introduces us, never hinting I'm Dad's daughter. Just her friend. Something about that feels nice.

"Jessica's a photographer too," she says.

"I'm just starting," I say apologetically. "I've never had a show."

"You might, though," Dana says. "If you win the contest."

Her friend encourages us to look at her work, and we do. I move from one to the next, taking them in. Her subject is paper. Crumpled paper, blank paper, paper written upon, torn paper, wet paper. Each one holds rich emotion: sadness, emptiness, hope, loss. Who knew so much lived inside something as mundane as paper? Artists can find meaning in the most unlikely places. I am very impressed.

Driving home, I realize my mood has lifted. In the time we were at the opening, I forgot how bad I was feeling. I turn to Dana.

"You don't have to be nice to me to get me to like you," I say.

Dana knits her brow. She glances at me. "Is that what you think I'm doing?"

"What are you doing, then?" I say.

"I took you to the opening because I thought you'd like it," she says.

"I did," I say. "A lot. It's just . . ." I take a breath. "We both know I haven't been the kindest person to you. To anyone, for that matter."

"You mean the comment about the kind of girls your dad likes?" She laughs.

"Among other things," I say.

"That didn't bother me in the least."

I watch out the window as we pass storefronts. The darkness zips past. "I wish I could just be like everybody else and accept the way things are."

I can feel Dana look at me again. "You can't," she says. "You see things too clearly."

I turn to look at her. Her profile is lovely. I can see more and more why Dad loves her. "I do?"

"It's an artist's curse," she says. She smiles. I get it. She has it too.

"Nobody else can stand it," I say quietly. I close my eyes, hoping she knows what I mean.

"Give it time," she says. "People come around."

The following week I come home to the familiar prattle from the living room. Mom's book group. This time I slip up the stairs. I don't want a repeat of last time.

The phone rings, and I pick it up.

"I have to be with you," Ted says. I swallow something hard in my throat and close my door.

"I can't," I tell him. I sit on my bed. Laughter erupts from downstairs.

"Why not?" he asks. "We were good together."

I rub at a hole in my jeans. "No," I say. "We weren't." I can't tell him the real reason. That I'm only fourteen, too young for what happened.

"You understood me," he says. He sounds sad and defeated. An old balloon. I can't even remember what I found attractive about him.

"There are plenty of girls out there," I say.

"Not like you."

I bite my lip.

"You can't keep calling me," I say. "Or coming around."

He doesn't say anything.

"It's over," I say.

"You're breaking my heart," he says. His voice cracks.

"You don't even know me." I wish I could tell him. Now would be the time. But I'm too scared of the consequences, of what he might say.

"Please," he says.

"I have to go," I say.

"Don't," he says, and I hang up.

I lie on my bed, looking up at the ceiling. His need hangs around me in the air like cobwebs. So does my lie, my frustration with myself for what I've done. If I could somehow capture it on camera, the desperation and longing, the regret and confusion, all the feelings strung together, I would have my photo for the contest.

When I come home from school the next day, Anne is watching TV in the family room.

"Didn't you go to school?" I ask.

She doesn't turn from the TV. It's a soap opera. Anne never watches TV. She's always reading.

"Who are you?" I say. "And what did you do with my sister?"

Anne just shrugs.

"Anne," I say. "Answer me. What's going on?"

"The answer is no," she says. "I didn't go to school." She glances at me quickly, then back at the TV. "Are you happy now?"

"No," I say. I stare at her, disbelieving.

"You seemed content before to make assumptions about how I was spending my time," she says sharply.

She's right. But this I didn't see coming. Not from miles away. I have to laugh. "How could you not go to school? You, Miss Perfect Daughter?"

Anne smiles a little.

"Oh, my God," I say. "You did something bad."

She still says nothing.

"You're killing me here," I say. I throw my bag on the floor, plop down on the couch beside her, and grab her arm. "Speak!"

She looks at me, that little smile still there.

"I spent the day with a boy," she says in a quiet voice.

"You?"

"Don't look so surprised."

"Who?"

"A boy in school. We've been talking for a few months, and we decided to go to the planetarium instead of going to school." She giggles. I haven't seen her giggle in ages. "It was fun. I've never cut school before."

"Anne," I say. I'm still grasping her arm. This is Anne, the queen of all that's right and good. This is so unlike her. I don't know what to say. All this time I've been telling her to get her own life.

"He's really nice," she says.

I sit there, dumbfounded.

"What does he look like?"

"I don't know. He's okay, I guess. I haven't thought about it much. He's nice to me, and he's fun to be around. That's what I care about."

She nudges me, and says, "What?" She wants me to say something.

"Nothing," I say. "I'm just happy for you." Which is true. "What does Mom think?" I ask.

"I haven't told her yet," she says.

"Really?" Another surprise. I figured Mom was her best friend, like Elisabeth and Deb.

Anne shrugs again. "I wanted to keep this for myself," she says. She looks at me. "You know what I mean?"

"I do," I tell her, knowing exactly what she means. She looks back at the TV. I can't help but sneak glances at her. A sinking feeling sits at the bottom of my belly. All this time Anne's the one who figured out how to be loved. Dana was wrong about me. I don't see things clearly at all. I see what I want to see.

• • • •

Dana and Dad walk hand in hand through the empty house. A rectangle of sunshine slants through a floor-to-ceiling window onto polished wood floors.

"It's perfect," Dana whispers.

They have taken Anne and me to the house they are considering buying. We stand by the wall, feeling like third wheels. Mom once told us about when she and Dad bought their first house, just after they were married. They found it through Mom's cousin, a realtor who had introduced Mom and Dad. He had gone to college with Dad. Mom said the house was small, but they called it their love shack. Anne was already forming inside Mom then, though they didn't know it. Now here's Dad with someone else. It's a wonder he can do it again without being jaded.

"It's a four-bedroom," Dad says. "Are you sure it's big enough?"

"The master, one for Anne, and one for Jessica." Dana smiles at him. "And one for one more."

Anne and I look at each other, surprised.

"A baby?" she whispers. We never even thought of that.

"I guess," I whisper back. I imagine a new, perfect little person. Nothing weighing her down. "Maybe it wouldn't be so bad."

Anne looks doubtful. "Mom would freak," she says.

I sigh. She's still so attached to Mom's feelings. I don't say anything, though. I look at her differently now that I know she has a boyfriend. My high horse has lowered considerably since I found out.

"Should we put a bid on it?" Dad asks.

Dana nods, the smile still on her face. She turns to look at Anne and me.

"I want to show you something," she says, and motions for me to follow. We go past the kitchen and downstairs to the basement. It is concrete and damp, like any other basement. It smells like mold. I don't understand why she's so eager to show me this. Then she opens a sea green door. A small room the size of a walk-in closet is on the other side. Shelves line the wall.

"A pantry," I say, confused.

"Now it's a pantry," Dana says. "I was thinking it could be a darkroom in a few months."

I cover my mouth, then my eyes. I don't want Dana to see me cry.

"You don't have to do that," I say once I've gathered myself.

"And you don't have to keep telling me 'you don't have to' whenever I do things for you."

I look around the room, imagining it red-lit and smelling of chemicals. I imagine myself in there, watching pictures take shape. Nobody's ever done anything this nice for me.

Dad and Anne come down the stairs. Dad lowers his head to clear the ceiling over the stairs. He meets my eyes and grins.

"You found out Dana's surprise?"

I nod, and Dana moves into Dad's extended arm. For the first time I don't feel uncomfortable as they kiss. Maybe it's because Dana isn't just the woman Dad left Mom for anymore. She's not some dirty secret, which is what I used to think. As we climb the stairs, I feel hopeful, like I can leave behind the Jessica who did too much with boys. Start again in this new house. Funny how things change. Suddenly I'm the one with something shameful to hide.

CHAPTER 12

A sneaker squeak echoes across the gym. Mr. Dalton, our gym teacher, has split the girls into two groups. One will jog the perimeter of the shiny tan floor. The other will practice the long jump on mats. I'm sure Elisabeth is thrilled she gets to run. She still won't even look at me. Not like I try to get her to anymore. I wait in line to jump over the tape on the floor. Ashley waits in front of me. She, like most people I used to be friendly with, hasn't talked to me since the thing with Josh. I'm trying not to let it get to me. Ashley's tied her white tee into a knot so her flat brown belly peeks above her green shorts. Only she can make our required gym uniform look sexy. In front of her is Tiffany. Tiffany, with her huge breasts and wide hips. She pulls at the back of the shorts, which keep creeping up her behind. Only she can make our uniform look cruel.

Mr. Dalton whistles as he sends Tiffany into her jump. With a running start she leaps off the ground, landing farther than anyone else. Mr. Dalton raises his eyebrows, clearly impressed.

Tiffany stands up and walks to the back of the line. When she senses me watching her, she glares back at me. Her laugh comes back to me: *You think they're your friends?* I look away. I can't help but remember fourth-grade gym class, where Tiffany's reputation started. We were playing soccer on the field when one of Ashley's friends noticed the large brown spot blossoming on her behind. She ran inside, her hand over her butt. Her breasts, still small and new at that time, bounced as she ran. Any hopes she might have harbored of being accepted were dashed. Only last year did kids stop calling her Stain.

In the middle of this memory something dawns on me, making its way across my body like another kind of stain.

I haven't gotten my period.

I've gotten my period exactly thirteen times, each exactly twenty-nine days apart. So where is it now?

My heart flutters against my throat. The gym goes kind of wavy and gray. I tell Mr. Dalton I have to use the bathroom, and run into the locker room, where I left my book bag. In the front of my notebook is a calendar. I

count back from today, my heart so loud I'm sure someone would be able to hear it if I weren't here all alone.

Today is the twenty-ninth day. I breathe out and head
right for the bathroom, knowing I'll see blood. I have to see
blood. I close the metal door and latch it. But when I wipe,
the tissue is completely clear.

In Spanish I can barely hear Senorita Clark's voice. I copy
the words from the board into my notebook, but they don't
register. After a moment I excuse myself to go to the bathroom. When I get there, there is still no sign of my period.
I tell myself to breathe deeply. It is normal for cycles to be
slightly varied. We learned that last year in Health.

When I get back to my desk, a few kids are giggling.
Ashley, in front of me, sits perfectly straight. I look down
and see what's so amusing. Ashley wrote SLUT on my notebook. Heat comes into my face. Then tears. I blink them
back, refusing to let anyone see me so bothered.

"Ha, ha," I whisper to Ashley. "Very funny."

When the bell rings, Ashley looks right at me. She
swings her highlighted hair over a shoulder and purses her
glossy lips.

"I wasn't trying to be funny," she tells me. She says this
seriously and not unkindly, like she wants me to listen.

I watch her go. Somebody bumps my back as he passes
me. It's Jason. He clears his throat and looks down. His dirty

blond hair is perfectly mussed, and he wears headphones around his neck. He has on a J. Crew turtleneck sweater.

"Excuse me," I say, hoping he hears the anger in my voice. After all, if it weren't for him and his perfect blond hair, if it weren't for the way that sweater hangs off his shoulders, showing off his gorgeous body, I wouldn't be in this mess.

Day 30 of my cycle, Ruth is in the hallway. I try to look busy, on my way to somewhere important, but it's no use.

"I was hoping I'd see you today," she says.

"I have some homework to catch up on," I say, "in the library." I gesture to the sea of people rushing by us.

"There's just a few weeks before the deadline," she says. She stares at me, concerned.

"I know." December fifteenth. The date's been etched into my mind, stuck there like a bad song. I still have nothing. Chances are I never will. I am tempted to tell her, let the truth come out: I no longer have a gift, like she once said. I'm just a pathetic loser who nobody likes. Worse, it's possible I'm a poster child for teen pregnancy. Won't that look nice in the contest bio.

"This week is Thanksgiving. I'm going to need something soon."

"I know," I say again.

Ruth gives a sharp nod, indicating she's starting to not trust me, and continues to her classroom. The girl with the painting, the one at the party whose name I never learned, walks by. She smiles, a small, kind smile.

"Do you have anything yet?" she whispers.

I shake my head. The hall is emptying as people disappear into classrooms.

"Maybe you're overthinking it," she says. "Sometimes I do that."

"What should I do?" I ask.

"Just do the first thing that comes to your mind."

"What if it sucks?" I ask.

"Then it sucks. And you do the next thing that comes to your mind."

I smile. She starts to leave, but I catch her arm. "I feel awful," I say, "but I don't know your name."

"Brooke," she tells me before she runs into Ruth's classroom, just making the bell.

The next day I bring some old photos with me, knowing I'll be staying late in the darkroom. Once I'm alone, I pull out the two photos I want. One shows me last year. I am laughing, my head tilted back. It is something I barely remember being able to do, laugh like that. Let it all go. So much has happened since to weigh me down. It feels impossible the girl in the photo is really me.

The next photo is recent, one of the ones I took a month ago when trying to capture my portrait for the contest. I can see the difference in my face. I am darker, more serious. My eyes are no longer so light. I lay the photos next to each other. Last year Ruth taught the class an overlay technique. You transfer the image of one negative to another. This is what I do with the two pictures.

A long time passes. Long enough that when I go out to the hallway for a drink from the water fountain, even the janitor seems to be gone. But when I come back and see the result, the time spent is clearly worth it. The old me hovers like a ghost over the new me. It is a picture of two girls, both me. A real self-portrait. I stomp my foot with a sense of finality. That's it. I'm done.

When I get home, I expect to hear it from Mom about being late for dinner, but instead I hear laughter from the dining room. I drop my bag and go to see. Mom, Anne, and a boy sit around the table, eating spaghetti. The boy is tall and skinny. He wears glasses like Anne, and I recognize him from the halls at school. All three look up at me.

"Jessica," Mom says. "Look who Anne brought home for dinner."

Anne blushes. The boy smiles a little. This must be Anne's boyfriend.

"I'm Lionel," he says. "Nice to meet you."

I smile. "Nice to meet you," I say. Anne beams at me. I'm not yet used to this blushing, happy Anne. Lionel goes back to eating. He cuts a meatball into four neat bites. He spears one and places it in his mouth. After chewing, he raises his fork to Mom.

"Delightful meatballs," he says.

I sit down, trying to hide my smile. I don't know what I expected, but it wasn't this. It wasn't Steve Urkel from that stupid TV show.

"Lionel is a junior like Anne," Mom says.

"Is that so?" I say, still working on not laughing.

Anne gives me a warning look. "Have some more salad," she says to Lionel. He smiles at her.

"She wants me to eat my vegetables," he says, looking at me. I can see he has some bad acne along his jaw. "She's so good to me." He reaches toward her, and they touch hands.

I raise my eyebrows, but when I glance at Mom, she looks only pleased.

"So," I say, hoping to change the subject. I don't want to see any more touching of body parts between these two. "What are your plans after high school?"

Lionel pats Anne's hand before pulling his back.

"College," he says. "Anne and I are talking about applying to Swarthmore together."

"You're planning your future together?" I blurt. I want to be nice, but they seem a little young for this. It's Anne's first boyfriend, and I doubt he was much of a Don Juan before Anne. I look again at Mom, trying to catch her eye, but she keeps smiling at Lionel.

"When you've found the right one, it makes sense," Anne says.

"Of course we both want to finish college before getting married," Lionel says. They nod at each other.

"How do you know it's the right one when it's the only one you've ever dated?" My voice is rising. I'm aware I'm being rude. I'm aware too my anger is misplaced. What am I really so pissed about?

Mom finally looks at me. "Jessica," she warns.

"Are you kidding me?" I say to her. "You think this is normal?"

Anne glares at me, the familiar darkness coming back into her face. I feel relief creep into my chest, but I ignore it. Do I really want my sister to be unhappy?

"Yes," Mom says. She looks at Anne and gives her an apologetic smile. "I think it's normal to want love in your life."

That's when I get it. It's not that I don't want Anne to be happy. It's that *I* want to be loved. Mom watches Anne with admiration, and Anne looks smugly at the both of us. Since when am I more like Mom than Anne is?

I sit back, my appetite gone. "Can I be excused?" I ask.

"You're not going to eat anything?"

"I'm not hungry," I say. I force a smile at Lionel, who stands as I leave. "Nice meeting you," I mumble.

"The pleasure was all mine," he says.

120

CHAPTER 13

The following day I go straight to Ruth's classroom with my photograph. If I can't have love, I can at least be Ruth's gifted student again. A promising young photographer of the future.

When I pull the photograph from its folder, Ruth lays it on her desk and stares at it. I watch her face, desperate for some sign of pride. When she doesn't say anything for what seems like a full minute, I feel like I might burst.

"It's an overlay," I say. "Like you taught us last year."

Ruth nods. "I see," she says.

I can feel my body deflate.

"You don't like it," I say.

Ruth looks at me. This close, I can see the soft fuzz on her cheeks. Her eyes are dark and warm. "I like it," she says. "But I've seen better from you."

121

My throat contracts like it does when I'm going to cry.

"It's the best I can do," I say. The tears pop into my eyes. I try to blink them away before she can see. "I don't have any other ideas."

Ruth puts her arm over my shoulder and pulls me to her. Even though she smells like incense, even though any kid passing by and seeing would tease me about it for years, she is warm and soft. I close my eyes.

"I see this has been a rough year for you so far," she says in a quiet voice.

I keep my eyes closed and lean against her.

"You have a story to tell about it," she says.

I take this in, my eyes still closed. After a few moments Ruth gently pulls me away from her, and with her hands on my shoulders she looks into my eyes.

"That's where your self-portrait is," she says.

I nod, understanding. I've been looking in the wrong place this whole time.

Tiffany and I are on the last late bus before we leave for Thanksgiving break. I sit all the way in the back corner this time. I don't want her to talk to me again. She sits near the front, but after we start moving, she gets up and walks toward me. She sits in the seat directly in front of me. Then she turns around and rests her arm on the back of the seat, facing me.

"What," I say.

"Don't worry," Tiffany says. "I'm not going to tarnish your glowing reputation with your friends."

I look out the window, my mouth set.

"I just wanted to apologize for what I said last time."

"Really."

"Really," she says. "I shouldn't have said it."

I'm not sure what to make of it, so I don't say anything.

Neither does she. Then she says, "You can't let them get to you."

"I don't know what you're talking about," I lie.

"Ashley and the rest," she says. "I once read there's some study showing that people like Ashley are less likely than people like you and me to be happy because they don't have to learn to cope."

"I'm not like you," I blurt. Immediately I wish I hadn't said it, because Tiffany looks surprised, then hurt.

"Fine," she says, and she gets up to go back to the front of the bus.

Thanksgiving morning Dad beeps the horn. I shake out my hair and put on my coat. Anne and I slide into the backseat. Dana and Dad smile at us from the front. Like every other Thanksgiving, we're going to Dad's parents in upstate New York. This year, though, Mom closed herself off in her bedroom when we left, and Dana's the one in the passenger seat.

"How is everyone?" Dad asks.

"Fine," we both say. We don't say anything about Lionel. Or the fact that my period is officially four days late. Or that I have been off course with the contest and now I have only two-and-a-half weeks to come up with something.

Dad smiles. "Good," he says. Of course.

At Grandma and Grandpa's we sit around the table. Dad's brother and his family are there. They are nice to Dana, but his wife keeps cocking her head at Anne and me like we need sympathy. Grandma is excessively chatty. She slips Anne and me each a fifty-dollar bill. Grandpa sits quietly, saying nothing. I never before had an opinion either way, but I'm starting to think I don't like this side of my family. Mom's side may be emotional, but at least they *have* emotions. These people are like wax replicas.

Dana is polite, but I can see she feels the same way.

On the ride home she turns to Dad.

"Now I understand," she says lightly.

"Uh-oh," Dad says. He's smiling.

"You're just doing what you learned," she says.

Anne and I look at each other. Nobody talks to Dad like this.

"What are you talking about?" Dad asks. He fiddles with the heat. He adjusts the rearview mirror. But he waits for her response.

"Nobody talks in your family."

Dad laughs. "What do you call what my mother did all the way through dinner?" He puts a hand on Dana's knee. "I don't think she knew what to make of us."

"That's what I mean," Dana says. She puts her hand over Dad's and entwines her fingers with his. The diamond on her engagement ring catches the light. "Nobody talks about what's really going on."

We are all silent. I can feel Anne next to me, neither of us moving a muscle.

"That's true," Dad says finally.

Dana puts her other hand over the one she's holding. I remember what she said after the gallery about nobody liking how I can't accept things the way they are. *People come around,* she said. I guess she was talking about Dad. Even though it can be uncomfortable at times, Dad appreciates her way of looking at the world. I look out the window at the bare, bony branches of the trees. The sky is darkening. It's that time of day I love, when everything shifts, showing something new. In the back of my mind I know Dad must like that about me, too.

When we get home, Mom is at the kitchen table.

"How was it?" she asks. She's got that fragile thing in her voice that tells me she doesn't really want to know. I throw my coat over a chair and go to the fridge for a drink. I'm not interested in getting pulled into her drama.

"It was weird," Anne says.

Mom perks up. She's wearing sweatpants and slippers. I wonder whether she even left the house today. "Oh?" she says.

"We missed you," Anne says.

Mom turns her mug of tea around and around. "Really?"

"Of course," Anne says.

I pour some juice and lean against the counter as I drink. Mom looks right at me, hopeful. I roll my eyes and put my glass in the sink.

"You know where I stand on the matter," I tell her.

She takes a sip of tea and says nothing. After a moment she looks back at Anne. We have an understanding now, I guess. I won't accept her crap, and she'll still love me, even though she doesn't like it.

I let the nurse lead me through the doors to a long fluorescent-lit corridor. The nurse is small and dark-skinned. She puts a gentle hand on my elbow when we reach the room. She smiles kindly and motions for me to sit. An examining table with stirrups sits in the center of the room. A clock ticks loudly on the wall. It smells sharp and sterile, like the color white. The nurse sits across from me with a clipboard.

"I'm just going to ask you a few questions, Jessica," she says. "And then we'll do the test."

I swallow. "Okay," I say.

"Age?"

I hesitate. "Fourteen," I say. But the nurse doesn't flinch.

"How long have you been sexually active?" she asks.

"It was only one time," I say. A nauseous feeling creeps along my skin. I cross my legs, then uncross them again.

The nurse smiles at me. "Okay," she says. "Are you monogamous right now?"

I look at her. I don't know what she means.

"Are you having sex with more than one person?"

"No," I say. I twist my hands in my lap. They're sweaty and nail bitten. I don't want the nurse to think I'm a slut, that I sleep with anyone. "It was just the one time," I say again, trying to make her understand.

"Were you using birth control?"

I shake my head and look down. My thighs spread on the chair. I cross them once more. I feel awkward and ugly, like I'm taking up too much room.

"Have you thought about getting yourself onto some birth control?" She is looking right at me now. Clearly this isn't a question on her form.

"I didn't know I was going to need it," I say. I don't mean to sound defensive. The whole situation happened so fast. I want her to understand.

"That's fine," she says.

I bite my lip, just wanting this to be over.

"Date of your last menstrual period?"

I calculate the date.

"Okay," she says. She hands me the small plastic cup on the counter. "You can use the bathroom at the end of the hall."

I hold the cup in both hands. This is it, the moment of truth.

"Jessica," she says. She leans forward. Her eyes are brown and pretty. "If it turns out you are pregnant, you aren't alone. We're here to support you."

I look down, tears in my eyes.

"Okay," I say.

She puts a hand on mine. Her hand is warm and soft. "No matter the outcome, you're going to be all right," she says.

"Okay," I say again.

Afterward I sit in the waiting room. My heart won't settle. It feels like it might jump right out of my body onto the floor. The clock on the wall says only three minutes have passed. The nurse told me they would know in five. I gnaw at a hangnail. The girl across from me is flipping through a *People* magazine. How can she be so calm when my whole world is being decided behind those doors? I haven't let myself think about what I would do or, worse, who I would tell. I look up. Six minutes. What are they doing back there?

I think of Ted. How could I not? He's probably at work right now, his heart perfectly calm. His heart probably has no reason to batter against his chest, banging and banging like an insistent knock.

"Jessica?" The nurse stands at the door with that damn clipboard. She smiles. Does that mean the test is negative?

I follow her, my legs as thick and heavy as wooden posts.

In the small room she smiles at me.

"I won't keep you waiting," she says. "Your test was negative."

I breathe out. My body lightens.

"But if your period doesn't come in another week, we should test again."

"Thank you," I say. I move to leave.

"One more thing," the nurse says. She hands me a small brown paper bag from the counter. "It's condoms," she says.

I look down. "I don't need them," I say, hating that I sound defensive again.

"That's fine," the nurse says. "But in case you do."

Monday the school is buzzing with excitement. It seems the principal brought in a sex educator from Canada to talk to us about birth control. We all skip third period to gather in the gymnasium. I can see Anne and Lionel near the front with the other juniors. I do my best to be invisible. I don't want anyone thinking about the parties and what I did with Jason and Josh.

The sex lady is older, at least Mom's age. She has graying hair and glasses. Her body is square and stout. I guess I expected someone young, maybe someone sexy. I hear mumbling. Others are surprised too. She puts a well-worn cardboard box on a table and hooks up a laptop to the projector. A big screen is already pulled down behind her. Someone dims the lights. I hear some giggling. Then a clinical drawing of a penis lights up the screen. The room goes quiet, and the sex lady starts talking. For some reason, I think of the retarded boy's penis I saw so long ago. I've seen two since then, but this is the one that pops into my mind. I squeeze my eyes, willing it to leave.

After a bit she changes the slide to show girls' reproductive organs. Then the real show begins. She dumps out the box and lines up various objects: a condom, a diaphragm, a packet of pills. I recognize them all from the book Mom gave Anne and me, and, of course, from the clinic. The snickering and whispering get louder, and teachers shush the room.

Just then I see Elisabeth. She is looking right at me.

"What?" I mouth.

But I know what she's thinking. She's thinking about

those pictures of Ted. She's wondering what I already know about sex, and about the gulf between us that keeps expanding. She's wondering if it's even possible to cross it, now that the gulf's grown this big.

After school I take the bus to the mall with the money Grandma gave me. My thought is if I get some new clothes, maybe I'll feel different. Better.

As I'm riffling through tops in Wet Seal, someone catches my eye. It's Tiffany. I look back at the colorful shirts quickly, but she's already seen me.

"Are you following me or something?" she asks. She's holding a pair of jeans with rhinestones sewn along the pockets.

I snort. "You wish."

There's a guy with her, a huge guy with a shaved head and a bull-ring in his nose. I don't recognize him. Tiffany sees me looking.

"This is my boyfriend, Nash," she says. "He's a senior at Bergen High." The public high school in town.

I shrug and look back at the shirt I've pulled from the rack. It's a revealing turquoise half shirt. I push it back between the others, hoping Tiffany didn't see it. I don't want her to think I would dress like that. And I don't look back up, because I also don't want her to keep speaking to me, although I can't believe she's talking to me at all after I was so rude on the bus last week.

"I don't get you," Tiffany says then.

I shrug again, my heart batting against my ribs. "What's to get?"

"We used to be friends," she whispers.

I swallow, unsure what to say. I keep flipping through the rack, but every single shirt looks stupid and ugly. I drop my hands to my side, anger rising suddenly and uncontrollably into my throat.

"You're the one who ruined it," I say.

Tiffany cuts her eyes at me. Her dark hair catches the fluorescent lights from the store. I know we're both remembering the party in sixth grade, where she let every boy there touch her breasts. This was the party that had clinched the deal for her, where she earned her status as the school slut. After that party, and after everyone in school knew what she had done, I avoided her in the hallway and wouldn't take her phone calls. When Mom asked why I wouldn't talk to her, I made up some story about how she had betrayed me. Of course, it was me who had betrayed her, left her alone with no friends. That's when Elisabeth and I started spending more time together. I knew what I had done was crappy, but my friendship with Elisabeth helped me forget the guilt. And, soon enough, things seemed like they had always been this way. Ashley and her friends at the top,

Elisabeth and me one step down, and Tiffany way at the bottom.

I bite my lip, seeing clearly now how that all worked out.

Nash puts an arm around Tiffany, pulling her toward him. For a brief moment I feel happy for her that someone wants to keep her safe. But Tiffany pushes him away. Her face is pinkish, and her eyes are slits.

"Do you really think I wanted all those assholes to touch me?"

I stay perfectly still, what she just said hovering around us like smoke. Like bad perfume. Of course she didn't want them to touch her breasts. How could I have been so stupid? A feeling I don't recognize is making its way up my body, moving through my feet to my legs.

Tiffany throws the jeans she is holding on the floor. Tears pop into her eyes. She is waiting for me to say something.

"I'm sorry," I squeak. "I see now—"

"No, you don't," she says, interrupting me. "You're like the rest. You don't see anything." She grabs Nash, and they leave the store, arms around each other.

I don't move, the feeling now in my throat. I know what it is: Shame. Thick and horrible.

"Do you need any help?" I turn to see a salesgirl. She's not much older than I am, with hair dyed hot pink. She's not looking at me, and she looks bothered. I follow her eyes to the jeans Tiffany threw, which lie twisted and crumpled on the ground.

The next day Nash waits for Tiffany in an old Buick after school. Tiffany walks right by me and slides into the car. I can see them kiss through the dirty windows.

"Gross," I hear Ashley say to one of her friends. "Nobody wants to see that." They are standing near me.

"She should keep that to herself," her friend says.

"Why can't you just let her be for once?" I blurt. My chest feels tight. A lump sits in my throat. Ashley turns to see me.

"I'm sorry," Ashley says. "Did you say something?" Her friend looks on, her chin high.

"Tiffany may not be our friend, but she's a human being," I say.

"Oh, please," Ashley says. "Since when did you get all WWJD? You're the one who dumped her when she stopped looking good on your social resume."

"That's not true," I say quietly. Tiffany's voice chimes in my mind: *You don't see anything.*

"Besides," Ashley says, "why should I have to see her make out with her nasty-ass boyfriend?"

"So don't look," I say. *You don't look at anything else,* I think, but don't say.

"You're right," Ashley says. "I won't." She and her friend turn to go.

I get it. She won't look at me, either, if she doesn't want to.

After school I take my Canon and go to the park. I need some time to think, and my camera helps me see things clearly. I realize, walking with my hands stuffed in my pockets, I haven't done this in a long time. I haven't taken time to look through my camera without the pressure of getting something right for the contest. A bunch of kids run around the playground. One little girl in a striped scarf laughs as she runs, her hands in the air. I aim my Canon and *snap!* Another girl sits on a bench with her mother, drinking from a juice box. Her mother, though right next to her, looks lost in thought. *Snap!* I get that one too.

I walk on, holding my camera tight against my side. I see a familiar entrance into the woods, and my breath catches. It's the place I went with Ted. My legs feel heavy, but I force myself to go there, to see. Perhaps there's something there for me, some sign of what has happened to me over these past few months. Some keyhole into who I am now. The wind blows sharply against my face. I can hear the kids yelling on the playground and cars whizzing by on the highway nearby. The trees have lost most of their leaves, so I can see the spot where we were. Where I first let Ted take me too far. The smell of the woods—the dead leaves and pine—makes my head swim. I step into the woods, pushing branches out of my way. I hold up my camera and look. In the circular space of the lens is a barren clearing. There is nothing, only leaves and dead branches. It is neither beautiful nor horrible. It's just empty.

CHAPTER 14

In the bathroom I find blood in my underpants. They are my favorites, but I'm so relieved I don't even care if I have to throw them out. I lie in my bed, relishing the achiness in my pelvis. *Thank you,* I think, in case someone is listening. I decide it is time to make some promises to myself. I get out a piece of paper and write them down: no sex again until I feel old enough to handle it; no sex again without some serious protection; and no sex again with someone I don't really care for. I aim my Polaroid at the paper and take a picture. Then I open my drawer to find the last Polaroid I took, the pine needles from the park. I crumple that one and replace it with the promises. I doubt I'll need the reminder after what I've endured these past few months, but you never know.

I decide it is time to talk to Elisabeth. She is sitting by herself in the cafeteria. It is something I admire about her. Even with me out of the picture, she felt no need to rush to find new friends. She's loyal. She has principles. I can see that clearly now. She believed how I was behaving was wrong, and she couldn't be a part of it.

She has her biology textbook open, and she doesn't notice me standing there at first. When she does, her eyes widen.

"Can we talk?" I ask her.

She shrugs, and motions to the chair where I'm standing. "If you want," she says.

I sit. The cafeteria is loud and busy, but the room shrinks to just her and me. I want to get this right.

"I need to apologize to you," I say.

She bites her lip, watching me. I can tell by the worry in her forehead that I've hurt her, and she's scared of getting hurt again.

"I've been an awful friend," I say.

"I know," she says.

"And self-consumed."

"Yes," she says.

"I was lying to you," I tell her. "About everything."

She stays still, waiting. Her face is tight with concern.

"That guy in the photograph," I say. I can feel tears creeping up my throat. "I had sex with him."

I wait for her to say something. "Oh, Jess," she says.

I swallow back the tears. I don't want to be like my Mom here, making this about my feelings. I realize that's how it's been for a long time with Elisabeth and me. She's the shoulder, and I'm the one crying. "I shouldn't have done it," I say. "But I also shouldn't have lied to you about it."

Elisabeth starts to tear up now too. "Yeah," she says quietly.

"And that whole thing with Jason," I tell her. "I was choosing a boy over our friendship. I should have listened to you."

Elisabeth reaches across the table to take my hand. "I should have been a better friend too," she says. "But I didn't know how to help you."

"I didn't need you to help me," I say. "I just needed you to stand by me while I screwed up."

Elisabeth nods. "That's a hard one for me."

I smile. "I know," I say.

"I'm not good with change," she says.

"Maybe not," I say. "But you're a good friend."

"Well," she says, "so are you."

We get up to hug, not caring what other people might think. I hold her tightly, unaware until this moment just how much I missed her.

Dana wraps a glass in newspaper and places it in a box. She and Dad are moving this weekend into their new house, and today she is helping Dad get everything packed. Dad and Anne are at the store, getting more boxes. She hands me the marker to write on the box I just taped shut.

"There's something I need to say to you," she says. She's looking down at the glass she's wrapping. Her blond hair is in a ponytail, making her look young.

"Okay," I say hesitantly.

"I never told you or Anne I was sorry."

"About what?"

Dana closes her box and rolls the packing tape slowly along the top. "About the affair, what I did to your family."

I don't move.

"I know your mother was devastated. I would have been too."

"It's not a big deal," I say.

"Yes, it was," she says.

I look down at the word "kitchen" I just wrote on the box. What does she know about what it was like? I swallow.

"I'm so sorry," she says again. "I wish I could go back and change things."

I keep my eyes on the box, wanting her to go on. Wanting to hear, finally, what happened, why Dad did what he did.

"Robert and I were just friends for a long time. I was in a relationship too. When that relationship ended, your dad was there for me."

I look up at her, anger starting to boil. I don't like

thinking of Dad this way, but maybe it's time to get real. "So, Dad pounced when you were vulnerable."

"No," she says. "It wasn't like that. Your dad was a perfect gentleman. That's what I'm trying to say. I'm the one who pursued him, Jessica. It was my fault."

"But why?" I say. "You knew he was married."

"He was so kind to me," she says. Tears come into her eyes. "I was in such a bad place. Nobody had ever been so nice to me."

I look away again, angry at her tears. Why does she get to be sad right now, after everything I've had to go through?

"He stayed with me all night when I was afraid to be alone."

"I'm sure he did," I say. Now the tears are coming to my eyes. I angrily wipe them away.

"He stayed on the couch."

When I don't say anything, she says, "I shouldn't have pursued him when he was married."

"No," I say. "You shouldn't have."

"I've wrestled with it ever since."

"Poor you," I say. I can't meet her eyes.

"I understand if you're angry with me."

"Gee, thanks," I say.

"Once I got to know you and Anne, I was angry with me too."

"Must have been hard."

"Jessica," Dana says. "Please. I'm trying to explain here."

I glare at her. "Really?" I say. My face feels hot with rage. "Because you have no idea what it's been like for me." A million things spin through my mind. Ted. Tiffany. My almost pregnancy. Jason. Elisabeth. The contest. I squeeze my eyes shut, trying to make sense of what's in my heart.

"I know," Dana says.

"No," I say. "For once you don't know."

I stomp out of the room to the bathroom. The tears come freely. I watch them stream uncontrollably down my face. Anne's anger at Dad and Dana was enough for both of us. It freed me up, so I didn't have to be mad. But the truth is, they were happy and in love while the rest of us had to deal with the fallout. Mom was a blubbering mess. Anne had to take care of her. With Mom and Dad so taken up with their own feelings, I went looking for someone else, anyone else, to take care of me. It wasn't fair. I turn on the faucet and splash water on my face.

When I come out, Dad and Anne are home. Anne gives me a questioning look. I guess it's obvious I've been crying.

"What did we miss?" Dad says, feeling the weight in the air.

"Jessica and I were talking about some things," Dana says. She tries to catch my eye.

"Can we just keep packing?" I say. In the past I would have taken this opportunity to smooth over the tension between Dana and me, but for now I just want to stay angry.

Dana nods. Dad looks perplexed, but he doesn't say anything more.

I start working on a box in the living room. "I'll tell you later," I mouth to Anne. I pick up an ugly ceramic ashtray I made for Dad when I was in the second grade. Dad doesn't smoke, but he keeps the ashtray out for decoration. I wrap it in newspaper and place it in the box. I gather his CDs and a small stack of movie videos and place those in the box too. I look around at the empty room to see what's left. It will be nice to not have to come back here, where all the memories of Dad's betrayal of Mom live, memories of how Dad got to move on. In the corner I see one of my photographs hanging on the wall. It shows a woman applying lipstick at a cosmetic counter. I never noticed before the sexuality in the picture. How could I have given this to Dad? The woman's hip juts to the side, her lips pout. The lipstick is a deep shade of red. I go to get it, before Dad sees. I grab newspaper and wrap it. But just as I am about to hide it in my own bag, I stop. What good will it do? Dad will still think of women in the same way. It won't change that he was attracted to Dana and left Mom. It won't change that he chose a younger woman and has sex. I turn around and put the picture in the box. There's nothing more I can do.

I follow Elisabeth up the carpeted staircase. She keeps glancing back at me and smiling. An hour ago she called to tell me she had a surprise.

"What is it?" I say, for the fifth time.

Elisabeth swings open her bedroom door. "Voila," she says.

I gasp. Her walls are pale green. Sheer purple and green curtains hang in the windows. Her bedspread is a pretty purple with little mirrors along the top. The shelves hold books and CDs, but no dolls.

"Well?" she says.

"I can't believe it."

"I finally did it," she says.

"Lizzie," I say. I put my arm around her. Even though I've been pressuring her to redecorate her room for ages, a part of me feels sad, like an old, worn teddy bear has been thrown out.

"It's symbolic," she says. "I saw an *Oprah* about how your living space reflects what's inside. My insides were ready to face that things are changing."

I shake my head and smile. She is still Elisabeth, even if she's an Elisabeth who can accept change. "Very impressive," I say.

She closes the door behind us and sits on her bed.

"So," she says. "Are you going to share, or what?"

"What do you mean?" I ask, joining her on the bed.

"Jess," she says. "You had sex. The real deal. I need to hear what it was like."

I shrug. I don't really want to recount the awful day with Ted. I don't come off well in the story either. "What do you want to know?"

"Everything," Elisabeth says. She pulls a purple pillow onto her lap.

I stand and go to the window. I push aside the curtains. A couple bundled in winter coats and hats walks on the sidewalk with a stroller. The trees shiver in the wind. I don't want to tell Elisabeth everything. I don't want to tell her how I felt afterward, emptied out and full of regret. But I also don't want to keep hiding from her.

"It wasn't great," I say, still looking outside.

Elisabeth doesn't say anything.

"I mean, afterward I wished I hadn't done it."

"Oh," Elisabeth says.

I still don't look at her.

"Maybe if I had been ready it would have been better."

"Yeah," Elisabeth says. Then, "If you don't want to talk about it, you don't have to."

"No," I say. "It's not a big deal."

"But it is," Elisabeth says softly.

"Yeah," I say. She's right. I have to stop saying things

145

aren't a big deal when they are. I turn to look at her now.

She waits while I make my way back to the bed. I take the other throw pillow and hold it in my arms, like her.

"It was also pretty gross," I say.

Elisabeth winces. "Really?"

"And it hurts."

Elisabeth's eyes widen.

"A lot."

"That sucks."

I nod.

"So," she says. "Would you do it again?"

I consider this. "Only with someone I really loved. And only if I felt ready."

Elisabeth laughs. "Great," she says. "You sound like someone on *7th Heaven*."

I laugh with her. "Maybe everything we need to know we can find out from bad TV shows."

"Or after-school specials."

I touch one of the mirrors on the bedspread. "Seriously, though, Liz," I say. "Don't make the same mistake."

"I won't," she says. She puts a hand over mine. "And you won't again either."

"I know," I say.

That weekend before the contest deadline the school holds an evening meeting. Apparently, some parents are pissed

146

about the woman who showed us condoms. The principal had a daily line of angry parents outside his door, so he decided to let everyone express their feelings at once. Mom wraps a scarf around her neck and reapplies lipstick in the foyer at home.

"I'm going to make sure the other side gets heard," she tells Anne and me before leaving. She looks right at me. "That our kids need access to information. You're going to get involved sexually whether we want it or not."

"Mom," I say, annoyed. I know, though, she's thinking of Mr. Gibbons at our door. She still never heard the truth about Ted.

"It's natural to have sexual feelings at your ages," she says.

Anne and I look at each other, uncomfortable.

"Just go, Mom," I say. Finally she does.

When she leaves, Anne is watching me. I wait, knowing she has something to say.

"Have you had sex?" she asks finally.

I feel my face twitch.

"Have *you*?" I say. "You're the one with the boyfriend."

"Jessie," she says. "Just answer me. I won't tell anyone, I promise."

I lean against the wall and cross my arms.

She looks at me, considering. I keep my eyes on the couch in the next room.

"I want you to feel like you can come to me," she says.

I nod.

"You're my sister," she says.

"Okay."

We stand in the foyer, looking at each other. Neither one of us knows what to say next.

"Okay," I say again.

Anne waits.

"I'm not going to do anything stupid," I say. I mean it. From here on.

"I'm glad," Anne says.

"I just want things to be good again." I feel like I'm about to cry. I blink, surprised at my emotion.

Anne steps toward me. "I'm sorry," she says. She puts an arm around me. I don't know what she's saying sorry for, but I think it's for all the things she knows I'm not telling her. We hug a moment, then we pull away. We're not used to expressing affection for each other.

"So am I," I say.

Anne and I are watching a movie in the family room when Mom comes home a few hours later. She sits between us, smelling of wintry air and her perfume. She puts her arms around us and pulls us close.

"Promise me you'll be safe," she says.

"We will, Mom," Anne says.

"I couldn't stand it if anything happened to you girls."

"Nothing will happen," Anne says.

"Jessica?" Mom puts her head against mine so I can feel the warmth of her cheek.

"What," I say.

"I need you to promise too."

"Fine," I say. "I promise. Happy now?"

I sound annoyed, but I close my eyes, letting her hold me a few more minutes.

"Yes," she says adamantly. "I am happy now."

CHAPTER 15

Two days before the contest deadline, I call Ted.

"I need to tell you something," I say. I take a deep breath, gathering my courage. This is my version of redecorating, of making my outside reflect my insides.

He is silent, waiting for me to explain.

"You're not going to like it."

"Come on, Jessica," he says. "You call after weeks of avoiding me to say something. What is it already?"

"It's about my age." I hold the phone tight. The upstairs hallway is empty and quiet. I waited to do this until no one was home.

I hear him breathing. "What about your age?"

"I'm not quite eighteen."

"How old are you, then?" He sounds angry already. I figure I better just get this out.

"Fourteen," I say quietly.

"Jesus," he says. I hear something bang on the other end of the phone. "I asked you. More than once."

"I'm sorry," I say.

"Were you trying to get me in trouble?"

"No," I say.

"I could go to jail, for God's sake."

"I know."

"What the hell were you trying to do?"

"I don't know," I say, though I do. I wanted his attention. I didn't want him to go away. This sounds so awful, though, so selfish. So I don't tell him. Some things are just mine to contend with.

"Jesus," he says again. "Why am I still talking to you? You're just a child."

"I'm really sorry," I say again.

"A sick child," he says.

I say nothing.

"Don't call here again," he says before he hangs up.

I put the phone in its cradle and go into my bedroom. From my window I can see it's starting to snow. Little flurries floating like dust to the ground. What is it about snow that quiets the world, so we have to stop and listen hard to hear? In the silence I think of Tiffany. I think of her dark shiny hair reflecting light in the store. I squeeze my arms around my middle. I wish more than ever I hadn't turned from her when she needed me, back in sixth grade. I watch the flakes as they fatten and fall faster. The ground outside slowly blurs beneath the whiteness. Because of course she was right. She and I are exactly alike. And I haven't been seeing a thing.

The following afternoon I am in the darkroom. It will be my last effort to have something ready for the contest. Then I will let it go. I do not have to be the best teenage photographer in the nation. I do not have to be Ruth's gifted student. I need only to take pictures. And to take the best pictures I can. I prepare the contact prints from the roll I took at the park. I dip them one by one. Then I dip the photos of the clearing in the woods. The image of the empty space fades into the room. Even though it's exactly the same spot, it looks so different from the photos I have of Ted on the blanket, the ones I took the day we were there together.

Then my idea for the self-portrait comes.

I gather up my things in a rush. I leave the new prints hanging there, too excited to wait for them to dry. I run to catch the earlier bus. All the way home I can't stop my leg from bouncing. I can't get there fast enough.

When I get home, I race up the stairs and pull out the

shoe box in my closet that holds my photographs. I flip through them until I find one of the two of Ted in the park. He looks out at me, a fierce, hungry look on his face. I turn on my computer and scan the photo. Then I get to work. I zoom in, again and again, closer and closer to Ted's face. I click closer until I am in the eye, and finally I see what I am looking for: me in Ted's eye.

Even with the camera up near my face, I can see the fear in my expression. The fish-eye effect distorts my body. I look small and flattened. I'm wearing a white bra and jeans. My shirt is off. My hair is tousled. I don't look anything like me. I kneel before him on the blanket, trapped in his gaze. I center the image, keeping his eye in the frame. This is it. This is my story. How could I have not seen this before? I am trapped in a man's gaze, my focus on him, no longer able to see myself.

I print out the photo. On the back I write my name, school, and grade, following the contest guidelines. Below this I write the title. My title. The title I took on just a few months ago: Slut.

Ruth is waiting for me when I arrive at her door the next day. It is December fifteenth, deadline day. She looks relieved when she sees me. She steps out from behind her desk and puts out her hand.

"Let's see what you've got," she says.

I wait as she pulls the photo from the envelope. She pulls a metal stool up to one of the drawing tables and places my picture on its surface. I grip my book bag, hoping she'll see what I see. I watch as she turns the picture over to read its title, then turns it back again.

Finally she says, "Oh, Jessica."

I raise my eyebrows, and she puts a hand on my arm.

"I see you here," she says.

"Yeah," I say. I can't stop smiling.

"For the first time all year."

"I know."

I turn to go to my first class, but Ruth calls my name.

"Thank you," she says.

"For what?"

"For having the courage to face yourself."

I smile again. I know exactly what she means.

EPILOGUE

And do you, Dana, take this man, Robert, to be your husband? To honor and cherish him, as long as you both shall live?"

Dana looks up at Dad. Her eyes are glistening with tears. "I do," she says.

Dad's been smiling since the beginning of the ceremony. I glance at Anne, who is standing next to me. Like Dana or not, she has to admit Dad's happier than he's been in a long time. Anne, sensing my gaze, looks back at me. She gives me a half smile. Maybe she's finally accepting this. When we put our bridesmaid dresses on and came downstairs, Mom surprised me by telling us how beautiful we looked. She didn't make one comment about hurt feelings or Dad. Maybe she's finally accepting it too.

And me? I shift my feet, uncomfortable in this fluffy gown. I'm finally accepting I don't have to like it all the time either.

I catch Elisabeth in the audience, trying not to laugh. She always laughs during emotional events. When I went with her to her grandfather's funeral, wanting to offer support, she laughed all the way through that service. It's her way of handling the emotion since her father died. We all have our ways of moving through pain, I guess.

I try to catch her eyes, but she's in a full giggle, her hand tightly over her mouth.

Next to her sits Brooke, who's become a good friend. She is shaking Elisabeth's arm, trying to get her under control. Brooke was thrilled with the photograph I submitted for the contest, and even more thrilled when I actually won. As a fellow artist she knew how much it meant for Summer Arts, the best arts camp on the East Coast, to offer me a full scholarship as a result of my win. Now she's coming with Dad, Dana, Elisabeth, and me when we go to D.C. in June for the gallery opening, only one month from now.

I wanted to invite Tiffany, too, but I knew she would have ignored me. We're still not friends. There's nothing I can do to repair that.

Finally Dad and Dana kiss, and we walk back down the aisle. Then we are forced to pose for a million pictures. Finally we are set free. I walk down a corridor into a large ballroom buzzing with Dad and Dana's guests. Tables are set with white linens and glowing candles. Funk is already blaring through the speakers. I search out Elisabeth and Brooke. Two days earlier, hanging out at my house, the three of us pinky swore we would stick with one another during the entire wedding. None of us wanted to get stuck alone at this thing. And none of us wanted to get stuck talking to Aunt Joan or Uncle Al for an hour.

Just as I find them, and as Elisabeth is about to make a snide comment about the dress, someone touches my arm. I turn around to see one of the cutest guys I've ever seen. Cuter than Jason ever was. Cuter, possibly, than any boy I've ever seen. He has curly brown hair. He's wearing a black jacket with no tie. When he smiles, he reveals two perfect dimples. Oh, my God.

"I saw you standing up there during the wedding," he says. I swallow. Why, of all times, must I be wearing this hideous dress? "My name's Cory."

I tell him my name. I tell him Elisabeth's and Brooke's names. They both smile and blush, clearly as awestruck as I.

"Would you like to dance?" he asks me.

Would I like to dance? I think. Um, that would be a yes.

But I glance at my friends. Their smiles are huge. They huddle against each other. If there's anything I've learned this past year, it's that my friends have to come before boys. I made them a promise, and I plan to stick with it. They have stuck with me, after all, even though I still have a reputation at school. Even though Ashley and her friends won't talk to them because of it.

"I think I'm going to just hang out here," I tell the gorgeous Cory. His smile lowers a bit. "I'm sorry," I add.

"What in God's name are you doing?" Brooke says when he walks away.

"There is no one at our school who looks like *that*," Elisabeth says.

"I know," I say. I watch him walk away. Wouldn't you know it? Even his walk is hot. "But I wanted to hang out with you guys tonight."

"You could hang out with us anytime," Brooke says.

I look at Elisabeth. "I'm with Brooke on this one," she says.

"Really?"

"Jessica," Elisabeth says, "just because you screwed up in the past doesn't mean you can't do things the right way now."

I hug Elisabeth. "Have I told you you're the greatest friends ever?" I say.

"Now go," Brooke says.

I spot Cory by the buffet. He has a plate in one hand. He's reaching for a stuffed mushroom with the other. I take a deep breath and approach. My heart is beating fast. This is different, after all. Like Elisabeth said, I'm going to do it right this time.

"Hey," I say when I get close.

He turns around, surprised.

"I guess I can do one dance."

"Oh," he says. He puts down the mushroom and the plate. "Okay."

We move out to the dance floor, where a bunch of other people shake their booties. Most of them are subdued, but a few are embarrassing themselves. I hope he doesn't actually want to dance, not when I'm wearing this dress.

"Who do you know here?" I ask.

"My mother is Dana's friend," he says. "They went to art school together."

"Your mother's an artist?"

He nods. His eyes are a deep blue. I try not to think about that, to focus on the conversation. That's a part of doing it right. "A photographer," he says.

I raise my eyebrows. "Wait," I say. "Did she just do a show on paper?"

"Yeah," he says, confused.

"I was at the opening," I say. "Dana took me." I smile. "She's my new stepmom."

He nods, getting it. "I couldn't go that night," he says. "I had a game."

"You missed your own mother's gallery opening for a game?" I tease.

"I see I shouldn't have," he says. "I missed an opportunity to meet you, as well."

I blush and look away. Brooke and Elisabeth stand near the buffet now. They wave. I smirk back at them.

"Why'd Dana bring you there, anyway?" Cory asks.

"I'm a photographer too," I tell him.

He laughs. "Just my luck. I find someone I think I like, and it's my mother."

I laugh too. "You don't know me well enough to know you like me," I tell him.

He raises his eyebrows. "Point taken."

The song fades, and another one starts.

"Well," I say, "thanks for the dance."

"That's it?" he asks. His smile falls again.

"We've got all evening to meet up again," I say.

I feel his eyes on me as I walk away.

For the rest of the wedding I laugh and dance and eat with my friends, forgetting he is even there. So when he comes back to ask for my phone number before he leaves, I am surprised. I write it on a cocktail napkin, and he stuffs the napkin into his jacket pocket. He reaches for my hand. My first reaction is to pull back. It will take me a while to get comfortable with a boy's touch again. To trust my body is safe in someone else's hands. When his hand finds mine, though, his touch is gentle. He pulls my hand to his lips and kisses it. The kiss is soft and warm. Enough to reach that silent self inside. The part that is slowly getting bigger. The part that is finally getting seen. He releases my hand,

and I smile, keeping my secret to myself. Keeping lots of things for myself these days.

As I return to my friends, a song we love starts, and we bounce out to the dance floor. With my friends I don't care what I look like dancing in this dress. I don't care that my hair falls halfway down as I shake my head to the music. I don't care that I'm probably offbeat. I'm letting my body do what it wants for once. No longer confusing that with what I think it *should* be doing, or what I think some guy thinks it should be doing. We laugh and clap and spin around. A flash pops, and I look up to see the photographer has taken a picture of us. I make a mental note—I'll want a copy of that photograph.

KERRY COHEN HOFFMANN is a psychotherapist who works with teens and their families. She received her MFA in creative writing from the University of Oregon and an MA in counseling psychology. A mother of two, she is a native of New Jersey but makes her home in Portland, Oregon.